God bless you

An Exegesis of the Revelation

by

W P Oakley

An Exegesis of the Revelation

ISBN 0-9665424-2-8

Published by The Master Design
in cooperation with Master Design Ministries
PO Box 17865
Memphis, TN 38187-0865
Info@masterdesign.org
www.masterdesign.org

Printed by Bethany Press International in the USA.

Table of Contents

Dedication

This book is dedicated to

Pattye Norman Oakley

My precious, devoted wife, lover, encourager, and best friend. Thank you for nearly fifty years of wonderful married life. Thank you for being my prayer partner.

And to

The memory of my dedicated father and mother, Dr. & Mrs. Willie B. Oakley, who are now with our dear Lord in heaven.

Acknowledgments

Through the encouragement and support of so many of my family and friends, this book has come to reality. It would be impossible to name everyone who has made a contribution to this project in one way or another. Yet, there are a few people who must be mentioned because of their colossal contribution to the completion of this work.

Without the help of Karen Droze Shafer, this production would have been much more difficult. She edited and typed the manuscript and then placed it on computer disk, ready for the publisher. She has also given assistance in many other ways. Thank you so much, Karen.

One of the finest groups of people in the world, in my opinion, is our Prayer Partner Board of Advisors for Mantle Ministries (the name the Lord gave us for our evangelistic and revival ministry). They are praying people who walk with Jesus daily. It was their prayers and so many other contributions that have been of immense help in bringing this volume to reality. These people are; Dr. Stan & Nancy Anderson, Hugh & Blanche Armstrong, Bernice & Marjorie Bolding, Ronnie & Monetta Campbell, Norris & Dean Cobb, Warren & Charlotte Cole, Rev. Jarrell & Reba Dawson, Karem & Libby George, Rev. Robert & Marcell Johnson, Jack & Pam Little, Jim & Cherry Lovelace, Dr. Jerry & Linda Muse, Gaylon & Vickie Sherrod, and Rev. Johnny & Susan Witherspoon.

Last, but not least, our deepest gratitude to S Faithe Finley, President of Master Design Ministries, who was of tremendous assistance and sweet patience as she guided us in all the details to print this book.

William “Bill” Oakley, D. Min.

Foreword

Very early in the ministry the Lord gave me a deep interest in the study of prophecy. In the pursuit of an education in college and seminary, that interest intensified to include not only prophecy but also Eschatology and where the books of Daniel and Revelation fit into the scheme of things. As my studies in these areas continued, my interests expanded to the study of Angelology and Numerology.

After almost fifty years of study and after reading over 250 volumes by many authors who approached the subjects from every conceivable theological viewpoint, I have come to a position on these subjects that is rich and meaningful to me.

Out of that background, it is a pleasure for me to share my heart in this little commentary on the Book of the Revelation from the pen of a Premillenialist.

Included in this volume is a short study of Numerology and a few notes on Angelology. May the Lord use it to inform, inspire and to cause us once again to "look for the coming of our Lord Jesus Christ."

William "Bill" Oakley

September 1999

The Meaning of Numbers

NUMBER 1
One is the symbol of unity and independent existence. One - unique, separate, set apart, alone. One is for God in the most hidden absoluteness of His being. It speaks of primacy, sufficiency, omnipotence. It speaks of harmony in all parts and attributes. It speaks of individuality and personality (Deut. 6:4; Zech. 14:9; Mark 12:32; Eph 4:4-6).

One - The personality and sovereignty and uniqueness, separateness and holiness of God.

NUMBER 2
Two means addition, an increase. So it pertains to help, to confirmation and to fellowship. Ecc. 4:9-12 - Confirmation and help. So in the Bible, 2 stands for testimony for confirmation.

Illustration of the use of 2 for testimony: When at a business meeting a man stands up and makes a motion and someone else stands up and says, "I second the motion," what is he doing? I second the motion. I am confirming his testimony. Two (2) is for confirmation and witness. There are 2 testaments, the old and new, by which God witnesses to man. The second person of the Trinity is Jesus, Rev. 1:5. Rev. 3:14, true witness. The second man, Jesus unites the 2 natures, divine and human, in His own person and He witnesses to us of men and of God. (John 8:17, Mark 6:7 - they might confirm each other in their witness and testimony to Christ (Luke 24:4; Acts 1:10).

NUMBER 3
Three is the number for divinity. Three is the Trinity of God (Matt. 28:19). Three is the symbol of divine, a complete, ordered whole. Three in one are these beginning, middle, end; Heaven, Earth, sea; father, mother, child; morning, noon, night; right, middle, left; knowledge, action, experience; body, soul, spirit; length, breadth, height.

Heb. 13:8, Gen. 18:1-2. Is not that significant? 3! Num. 6:24-26 - A threefold benediction; a threefold benediction is seen in the words sung by the seraphim in Isa. 6:3. Three times daily prayer (Psa. 55:17; Dan. 6:10).

Ex. 29:20 - Consecration of Priest and Lev. 14:14 - Cleansing of the leper, the blood is placed (the blood of sacrifice, consecration and cleansing) upon the tip of his right ear, upon his right thumb and upon the great toe of his right foot. The whole man belongs to God.

Relationship to deity:

Matt. 4:3	-	3 temptations
Matt. 16:21	-	Christ arose on the 3rd day
Matt. 26:34	-	Peter denied Christ 3 times
Matt. 26:44	-	3 prayers in Gethsemane

NUMBER 4

Four is the number of the world of God's creation. Four seasons, 4 directions, 4 phases of the moon, 4 elements, (Earth, air, fire and water), God's world, God's creation, God's universe.

Gen. 2:10 - River of Eden has 4 heads, divides into 4 parts, refers to God's sustaining care for His world.
Matt. 13:19-23 - 4 kinds of soil, 4 kinds of hearers.
Jer. 49:36 and Ezek. 37:9 - 4 winds, Rev. 7:1.

Four is the first number that can be divided by 2, a symbol of the weakness of the creature in contrast with the creator. It is a symbol of us in this world. It is a symbol of failure and of trial. The book of Numbers is the fourth book in the Bible and is a type of our pathway and trial in the wilderness of this world. This extends to the multiple of 4. 4 x 10 = 40 (40 refers to a time of trial and testing in the Earth). In the days of Noah, it rained 40 days and 40 nights.

Moses was on Mt. Sinai 40 days. Jesus was driven into the wilderness to be tempted of the devil 40 days - trial and temptation. We are tempted 3 ways - body, soul, spirit (Matt. 4:3-8).

NUMBERS 5 AND 10

They are together because they are of the same thing. Ten is integral in thinking of human life. The tithe is a tenth. All that we have is conceived of as being divided into 10 parts, of which one part belongs to God as a token of God's sovereignty. Ex. 29:20; Lev. 14:14 each connected with 5 which was mentioned earlier in number 3.

There are 5 senses by which we are in contact with the world. These are: 5 fingers on the hand by which a man executed his choice. There are 5 toes on his foot by which man walks. The basis of the decimal system originated in counting with the fingers. The full rounded man was the man who had all of his fingers and toes.

Five doubled to 10 came to stand for human completeness. The whole duty of man is summed up in 10 commandments. Rev. 13:1 - The 10 horns stands for complete power in human government. Dan. 2:41-42 - Ten stands for worldly, human completion. Matt. 25:1-13 - The 10 virgins represents the churches in their entirety, in their mixed and slumbering and earthly condition, some of them dead and sound asleep; some of them alive and vibrant and quickened. Luke 19:13 - The 10 pounds entrusted to 10 servants. The whole responsibility and sovereignty of God placed in our hands. Luke 15:8 - Ten pieces of silver representing all of the devotion of his life.

The multiples of 10 intensify the meaning of the basis number. Rev. 9:16 - An immense army; Rev. 2:10 also has meaning of being intense, fierce and intense tribulation; Ex. 7:12 - 10 plagues, terrific in the extreme.

Five also shows God acting in grace (Phil. 2:7,8).

NUMBER 6

Seven is the sacred number. Six falls short of it. It represents failure. It is the number of man. He was created on the sixth day. His workday week is 6 days. Hebrew slaves served 6 years. The darkness of the cross began at the sixth hour. Jesus was crucified on the sixth day of the week. It is the worst of all numbers. I Sam 17:4; Rev. 13:18; 666. Six units, 6 tens, 6 hundreds. Three sixes, three successively higher powers in the decimal scale. That is evil in its fullest activity. I Sam 17:4 - Goliath, 6 cubits and a span. Dan. 3:1 - Golden image, 60 cubits high and 6 cubits broad. Ezek. 39:1-2, all but 1/6 was destroyed. The number of a man vainly and impiously aspiring to be God; the deification of man; the dethroning of the Son of God. The antichrist whose number is 666 is a leader where labor is without prayer, where culture is without Scripture, where songs are without Psalms, where rules are without reverence. His is a world without God. Six means failure - shortcoming.

NUMBER 7

Seven is the sacred number and symbolizes the fullness and perfection of God's Word. The perfect world number is 4 — it represents the world. The perfect divine number is 3. Together they make the holy and sacred number 7. Seven is the Earth crowned with Heaven, the union of Earth and Heaven.

The seventh day was hallowed by the Lord after the works of creation, after the creative work of God. It speaks of fullness, of completeness, of accomplishment and of rest.

It is used at least 600 times. It means perfection, completeness, fullness and plenitude.

Rev. 1:4 - Of all churches
Rev. 5:6 - 7 horns - fullness and plenitude of power
7 eyes - He is omniscient. Christ is seen as all-powerful, all wise.

Uses of the 7. Ritual, Historical and Literary

Ritual Use:

Gen. 2:1-3 - Sabbath
Ex. 22:30 - 7 days old
Ex. 34:18 - 7 days
Lev. 16:14, 19 - 7-fold sprinkling of blood
Num. 8:2; Zech. 4:2 - Lampstand, 7 branches, 7 lights
II Kings 5:10 - Naaman dipped 7 times

Historical Use:

Gen. 7:4, 10 - 7 days of grace
Gen. 8:4 - Ark rested on the 7th month
Gen. 41:53-54 - 7 years of plenty and 7 years of famine
Josh. 6:8-16 - 7 priests marched around Jericho 7 days blowing 7 trumpets and on the 7th day they marched 7 times.
I Sam. 16:10 - Jesse's 7 sons
Solomon took 7 years to build the temple
In Matt., Luke and John - 7 words from the cross

Matt. 15:34-37 - 7 loaves; 7 baskets of fragments
Mark 10:9 - 7 devils cast out
Acts 6:3 - 7 deacons chosen

Literary Use:
Psa. 12:6 - Completely purified
Matt. 12:45 - 7 evil spirits
Luke 17:4 - Three things here: 7-fold sin, 7-fold repentance and 7-fold forgiveness
Matt. 6:9-13 - 7-fold petition, 7 petition in Model Prayer
Matt. 13 - 7 parables of kingdom - a complete view, a whole view of the kingdom of Heaven
Matt. 23:13-29 - 7 woes pronounced, wholly condemned

Multiples and division of 7

2 x 7 = 14. Ex. 12:6, 18 - Passover 14th of Nisan.
Num. 29:13, 19 - 14 lambs offered on each of the 7 days of the Feast of Tabernacles.
Matt. 1:17 from Abraham to Christ in the genealogy of the first chapter of Matthew there are 3 groups of 14 in each.
7 x 7 = 49. Lev. 23:15 after 49 days from the Passover was Pentecost. 7 weeks.
Lev. 25:8 - Jubilee is after 7 times 7 years (after 49 years) the 50th year was Jubilee.
7 x 10 = 70. Strong expression for multitude.
Ex. 1:5 - 70 members of Jacob's household.
Ex. 24:1, 9 - 70 elders of Israel.
70 members of Sanhedrin.
70 disciples sent to preach the gospel.
Gen. 50:3 - 70 days of mourning for Jacob.
Isa. 23:15, Dan. 9:2, Zech. 1:12 - 70 years of captivity.
Dan. 9:24 - 70 weeks of Daniel.
Psa. 90:10 - 70 years human life span.
Matt. 18:22 - 70 x 7 unlimited Christian forgiveness.
In Daniel and the Revelation we see the division of 7 again and again.
Cut in half (3 1/2) - the incomplete, the imperfect.
It is found in 4 different terms: 3 1/2 years, 42 months, 1260 days or time, times and half a time.
Luke 4:25 - 3 years 6 months (James 5:17).

Dan. 7:25 - Time times half a time 3 and 1/2.
Dan. 9:27 - One week 7 - Midst of week 3 1/2 days.
Dan. 12:7 - Time times half a time.
Rev. 11:3 - 3 1/2 years. Rev. 12:6 - 3 1/2 years.
Rev 12:14 - Time times half a time.
Rev. 13:5 - 42 months or 3 1/2 years
Rev. 11:9 - 3 1/2 days. Rev 11:11 - 3 1/2 days.

NUMBER 8

Eight is the member of the new order, the number of the new departure. A new beginning. There are 7 notes in the musical scale. The eighth note is but the octave, the beginning of the series in a higher key. .

It speaks of the new covenant, a new creation. Col. 2:11; Deut. 30:6 - Circumcision of heart; II Cor 5:17; Eph. 2:10 (Lev. 23:11 - 8th day, I Cor. 15:23). The sheaf of the first fruit is a type of the resurrection of our Lord. On the 8th day, on the morrow after the Sabbath, on the first day of the new week our Lord arose. It is a new day. It is a new covenant. It is a new gospel. It is a new creation. It is a new departure.

NUMBER 9

Nine speaks of divine completeness from the Lord. Significantly, it is three times three. Nine is the number for the Fruit of the Spirit. Nine comes after eight which represents the New Birth. The Fruit of the Spirit follows New Birth. In I Cor. 12:8-10 Paul mentions nine gifts of the Spirit.

In Matt. 5:3-12 there are nine Beatitudes which our Lord spoke in His Sermon on the Mount. These reveal what God wants us to be in the Divine Completeness of the Kingdom of Heaven.

It was the ninth hour that Jesus died on the cross, thus completing God's plan of salvation.

In God's direction to Israel concerning the Sabbath year (Lev. 25:2-4), they were told to make plans for their food (Lev. 25:20-22). This shows that in the Sixth, Seventh and Eighth years, they ate of what was planted the sixth year. In the eighth year they sowed again, and in the ninth year they began to eat of the fruit of what was sown in the eighth year. This represents the Fruit of the Spirit, represented by number nine, which follows the New Birth, represented by number 8.

Number 10

Ten means testimony and responsibility. Man has ten digits on his hands and feet. There were ten Patriarchs before the flood (Gen. 5). God gave ten commandments to man for him to bear testimony before God and man. There were ten plagues upon Egypt and Pharaoh during the days of Moses.

Ten powers become powerless against the love of God (Rom. 8:38).

Ten vices which exclude from the Kingdom of God are listed in I Cor. 6:9-10.

The tithe is a tenth of our earnings belonging to the Lord. The tithe is our testimony of faith unto the Lord.

Ten Psalms begin with Hallelujah (Psa. 106, 111, 112, 113, 135, 146, 147, 148, 149, 150). Here the Psalmist is giving his testimony of Praise unto the Lord.

Number 11

Eleven speaks of disorder and judgment. Eleven follows ten. Ten represents the law and responsibility. A broken law and responsibility always brings judgment and disorder.

There are eleven judgments upon the Egyptians:

1. Blood (Ex. 7:19-21)
2. Frogs (8:1-7)
3. Lice (8:16-17
4. Flies (8:21-24)
5. Murrain (9:1-7)
6. Boils (9:8-11)
7. Hail (9:22-25)
8. Locust (10:12-15)
9. Darkness (10:21-23)
10. First-born (12:29-30)
11. Overthrow at Red Sea (14:24-28)

Noah pronounced judgment upon Canaan, a son of Ham, because Ham saw his father's nakedness when he was uncovered in his tent (Gen. 9:20-25). In Gen. 10:15-18, it says that Canaan had eleven sons.

In Jer. 52:1 it is said that Zedekiah reigned eleven years in Jerusalem. He was a wicked king (v. 2). In verse 5, Jerusalem was besieged by the king of Babylon and judgment was given unto him (v. 7-9).

The eleven days journey across the wilderness brought the children of Israel to a place of judgment (Deut. 1:2), and they wandered in the wilderness for forty years.

There were eleven things John saw in connection with the Great White Throne of Judgment:

1. A great white throne.
2. Him that sat upon the throne.
3. The dead, small and great, stand before God.
4. The Books were opened.
5. Another book was opened - the book of life.
6. The dead were judged out of the things written in the books.
7. The sea gave up its dead.
8. Death and Hell delivered up their dead.
9. They were judged every man according to his works.
10. He saw death and Hell being cast into the lake of fire.
11. Those cast into the lake of fire whose names were not written in the book of life (Rev. 20:11-15).

NUMBER 12

Twelve means governmental perfection. This number is used as a signature of Israel.

Twelve is the number of Government by divine appointment (Matt. 19:28).

Gen. 17:20 states that Ishmael beget twelve princes.

Numbers 1:5-16 says twelve were named over the twelve tribes of Israel.

I Kings 4:7 says Solomon had twelve officers (princes) over all Israel.

There were twelve tribes of Israel to make up the nation.

Twelve spies were sent out by Moses to spy out the land of Canaan.

Elijah built an altar of twelve stones, and fire from Heaven came down and consumed the offering (I Kings 17:30-40).

Jesus chose twelve disciples to follow him.

Twelve comes after eleven. The reign of Christ and His saints will follow the judgment (11) of the false woman (Rev. 17:1 and 19:2) and the judgment (11) of the beast and his associates (Rev. 19:11-21). The account of this reign is found in Rev. 20:1-6. This account follows immediately after the prophecy of the destruction of the beast, his armies, and the kings of the Earth, as found in Rev. 19:11-21. Let the opponents of Premillennialism take the numbers and prove their point!

NUMBER 13

Thirteen speaks of depravity and rebellion. Jesus mentions thirteen things when He gave a picture of the Rebellion and Depraved heart of man (Mark 7:21-22).

The word Dragon, which is a symbol of the devil (Rev. 12:9), is found thirteen times in the Book of Revelation. The devil is behind all rebellion.

See Gen. 14:4.

In Esther 3:8-13, Haman, the enemy of the Jews, had a decree signed on the thirteenth day of the first month to have all the Jews put to death on the thirteenth day of the twelfth month.

See Num. 17:10.

Examine Num. 3:39-51 and you will find that the Lord took the Levites in exchange for the firstborn. The exchange was made person for person until the number of the Levites was exhausted. Then there remained 273 of the firstborn who had to be redeemed with five shekels per person. Divide 273 by 13, the number of Depravity and the result is 21. The number 21 stands for the exceeding sinfulness of sin. There are exactly 21 sins recorded against Israel from Egypt to Jordan:

1. Ex. 14:10-21	8. Lev. 10:1-2	15. Num. 15:32-36
2. Ex. 15:23-24	9. Lev. 24:10-14	16. Num. 16:1-35
3. Ex. 16:1-3	10. Num. 11:1-3	17: Num. 16:41-50
4. Ex. 16:19-20	11. Num. 11:10-35	18. Num. 20:1-6
5. Ex. 16:27-28	12. Num. 12:1-15	19. Num. 20:8-12
6. Ex. 7:1-4	13. Num. 14:7-11	20. Num. 21:4-9
7. Ex. 32:1-9	14. Num. 14:40-45	21. Num. 25:1-9

The thirteenth sin in the above list is where Israel rebelled and refused to go up and possess the land (Num. 14:6-9).

Number 14

Fourteen speaks of deliverance or salvation. It was the fourteenth day of the month when the children of Israel were delivered from Egyptian bondage.

The number fourteen is found three times over connected with Christ's coming into the world, and He came to save or deliver His people from their sins (Matt. 1:17).

Fourteen and three are often found together. Fourteen is deliverance and three is for resurrection. Israel was delivered from the plagues of Egypt on the fourteenth day. Three days later they passed through the Red Sea, which is a figure of Resurrection.

On his voyage to Rome, Paul and his company were caught in a violent storm (Acts 27:14-44). God sent His angel and told Paul all would escape alive (v. 22-25). There were 276 on board the ship (v. 37). In Rom. 1:29-32 we see 23 things mentioned that show the number of death. Twelve (Divine authority) goes into 276 exactly 23 times. They were saved from death in the storm on the fourteenth day (vs. 33-44).

Number 15

Fifteen means rest. Lev. 23:6-7; Lev. 23:34-35; Esther 9:20-22.

The fifteenth time the name Naomi is found is where she said the words of Ruth 3:1.

Number 16

Sixteen means LOVE. There are sixteen times in the Bible we find Jehovah titles (see I John 4:16). "God is love." Sixteen times the word "Jehovah" is combined with other words to make "Jehovah Titles."

1. Jehovah - Elohim = The Eternal One or Creator (Gen. 2:4-25)
2. Adonai - Jehovah = The Lord our Sovereign (Gen. 15:2, 8)
3. Jehovah - Jireh = The Lord will provide (Gen. 22:8-14)
4. Jehovah - Nissi = The Lord our banner (Ex. 17:15)
5. Jehovah - Ropheka = The Lord our healer (Ex. 15:26)

6. Jehovah - Shalom = The Lord our peace (Judg. 6:24)
7. Jehovah - Tsidkenu = The Lord our righteousness (Jer. 23:6)
8. Jehovah - M'kaddesh = The Lord our sanctifier (Ex. 31:13)
9. Jehovah - Sabaoth = The Lord of Hosts"(I Sam. 1:3 - used 281 times)
10. Jehovah - Shammah = The Lord is present (Ezek. 48:35)
11. Jehovah - Elyon = The Lord most high (Psa. 7:17)
12. Jehovah - Rohi = The Lord my shepherd (Psa. 23:1)
13. Jehovah - Hosenu = The Lord our Maker (Psa. 95:6)
14. Jehovah - Elohenu = The Lord our God (Psa. 99:5, 8, 9)
15: Jehovah - Elohekna = The Lord thy God (Ex. 20: 2, 5, 7)
16. Jehovah - Elohoy = The Lord my God (Zech. 14:5)

In I Cor. 13:4-8 there are sixteen things said about love. The sixteenth time Paul's name occurs is where he is called "beloved" (Acts 15:25).

NUMBER 17

Seventeen speaks of victory. This number is usually compounded in Scripture of the numbers SEVEN and TEN. Seven signifies completeness and ten signifies testimony, so the two combined have the deeper significance of "Testimony of Completeness" or Victory.

In Genesis Chapter 5, we have the seemingly dry details of the patriarchs ages. Methuselah lived 969 years. This age is divisible by seventeen. When he was 187 years of age, he beget Jamech which divides by seventeen. "Methuselah" means "when he is dead it shall be sent." Methuselah died just before the flood. Jamech's age after Noah's birth (595) can be divided by seventeen. So God, in the ages of these two men - one Methuselah, whose death signaled the judgment to come (the flood) - and the other, Jamech, of whom Noah was born, the godly man, to be preserved through the flood marked the significant number seventeen - VICTORY.

The day the Ark floated safely on the rising waters was the "seventeenth day" (Gen. 7:11) - and the day it came to rest on "Mount Ararat" was the "seventeenth day" of the seventh month (Gen. 8:4).

Jesus was crucified on the occasion of the Passover which was on the "fourteenth day of the month" (Lev. 23:5). He was resurrected three days later - making "seventeenth day of the month" when He arose VICTORIOUS over sin and the grave.

NUMBER 18

Eighteen means bondage (Luke 13:16, Luke 13:4-5, Judges 3:14, Judg. 10:7-8). In the Old Testament there are 18 places where "bondage" is spoken about.

1. Gen. 15:13-14	7. Ex. 6:9	13. Deut. 8:14
2. Ex. 1:14	8. Ex. 13:3	14. Deut. 13:5
3. Ex. 2:23a	9. Ex. 13:14	15. Deut. 13:10
4. Ex. 2:23b	10. Ex. 20:2	16. Deut. 26:6
5. Ex. 6:5	11. Deut. 5:6	17. Josh. 24:17
6. Ex. 6:6	12. Deut. 6:12	18. Judg. 6:8

The eighteenth time the word "Bondage" is found in the above list is Judg. 6:8. At the time the prophet spoke these words the Israelites were in Bondage to the Midianites. The eighteenth time Israel's bondage is referred to, completes the full number of times their bondage is mentioned. Now read Judg. 6:1. Since seven stands for completeness, then the time Israel was in bondage to Midian seven years completed the eighteen times their Egyptian bondage is mentioned. This last reference completed the number (eighteen) that stands for bondage.

NUMBER 19

Nineteen means faith. There are nineteen different persons referred to in Heb. 11:1-32. While the name of Joshua is not mentioned in verse 30, yet Joshua was the leader of Israel at the overthrow of Jericho.

1. We - Heb. 11:1	11. Joshua - v. 30
2. Abel - v. 4	12. Rahab - v. 31
3. Enoch - v. 5	13. Gideon - v. 32
4. Noah - v. 7	14. Barak - v. 32
5. Abraham - v. 8-10, 17-19	15. Samson - v. 32
6. Sarah - v. 11	16. Jephthae - v. 32
7. Isaac - v. 20	17. David - v. 32
8. Jacob - v. 21	18. Samuel - v. 32
9. Joseph - v. 22	19. The Prophets - v. 32
10. Moses - v. 23, 29	

Now look at the arrangement of these numbers:

> Moses - Number 10 (represents law)
> Abel - Number 2 (represents division)
> Enoch - Number 3 (represents resurrection)
> Noah - Number 4 (represents world)
> Abraham - Number 5 (represents grace)
> David - Number 17 (represents victory)

In Paul's discussion of justification by faith in Rom. 3:21 - 5:2, he used the word "faith" nineteen times.

Eph. 2:8 - "For by grace (5) are ye saved (14) through faith (19)."

Number 20

Twenty speaks of redemption. The males of the children of Israel had to offer a ransom for their souls at age twenty. The money that was given for their ransom was silver money. Silver is a symbol for redemption.

There were twenty boards on each side of the Tabernacle north and south (Ex. 26:18-19). The silver sockets were also mentioned in connection with each side. This represents a twofold redemption—a redemption for the body and a redemption for the soul.

In Ruth 4:1 10 there is the record of Boaz, the "kinsman redeemer" redeeming the property that was Elimalech's and Naomi's and purchasing Ruth to be his wife. The name Boaz occurs twenty times in the book of Ruth.

Jacob labored in the household of Laban for twenty years in order to redeem Rachel (Gen. 31:38-41).

Number 21

Twenty-one speaks of exceeding sinfulness of sin. The history of Israel's wilderness journey discloses that twenty-one sins were recorded against her from Egypt to Jordan.

In II Tim 3:2-5, Paul lists twenty-one things which men would do in the last days.

In Matt. 23, we have recorded twenty-one characteristics of a hypocrite:

1. Demand respect as teachers (v. 2)
2. Teach, but do not practice (v. 3)
3. Demand service, not give it (v. 4)
4. Seek praise of men (v. 5)
5. Parade their religion (v. 5)
6. Seek chief banquet places (v. 6)
7. Seek chief places in church (v. 6)
8. Glory in personal attention (v. 7)
9. Glory in titles (v. 7)
10. Rob men of truth and life (v. 13)
11. Reject truth and life (v. 13)
12. Take advantage of widows (v. 14)
13. Exhibit long prayers (v. 14)
14. Are zealous to win men to their sect, but not to God (v. 15)
15. Root and ground converts in hypocrisy, not in God (v. 15)
16. Prefer to be the only guide in Religion, but are blind to the truth (v. 16-22)
17. Propagate those parts of religion from which they receive most personal gain and honor (v. 16-22)
18. Strain at gnats and swallow camels - stress minor details and omit the fundamentals of religion (v. 23-24)
19. Glory in bodily cleanliness, but live in moral filth (v. 25-26)
20. Exhibit outward religion and self-righteousness and ignore inward holiness in life and conduct (v. 27-28)
21. Pretend to be more righteous than their forefathers (v. 29-33)

NUMBER 22

Twenty-two means light. There were twenty-two bowls to hold oil in the candlestick in the Tabernacle. There were three branches on each side of the shaft of the candlestick. Each branch had three bowls. In the shaft were four. Six branches with three bowls each make eighteen, and the shaft had four, making twenty-two.

In Acts 22:4-11, Paul was relating his experience on the Damascus road. He told about the great light that shone from Heaven. In this place the name of Saul occurs the twenty-second time.

In Num. 3:39, a total of 22,000 Levites were numbered to serve in the Priestly work of the Tabernacle. They were to give and minister light to the people. The number thousand means "Glory of our Lord" and twenty-two is the number of light. Thus, the 22,000 Levites were to reveal to the people the "Light of the Glory of the Lord."

The word "light" is found 264 times in the Bible. Divide that number by twelve (the number of Administration) and we have the number of light. In other words, we are to administer the light of the World to the hearts of people.

In the gospel of John the word "light" is used twenty-two times.

NUMBER 23

Twenty-three means death. Rom. 1:28-32 list twenty-three things that God said "they which commit such are worthy of death."

Ten represents the law, and thirteen the depraved, rebellious heart of man. (Sin through the law brings death: 10 + 13 = 23).

Rom. 7:9 - "I was alive without the law (10) once, but when the commandment (or law) came, sin (13) revived and I died (23)."

I Cor. 15:56 - "The sting of death (23) is sin (13), and the strength of sin is the law (10)."

Rom. 1:32 - "Who know the judgment (11) of God (12 - the Divine Judge), that they which commit such things are worthy of death (23)."

In studying the resurrection of I Cor. 15, Paul used the word "RESURRECTION" four times, "RAISED" ten times, "RISEN" three times, "RISE" four times, and "ROSE" twice. This is twenty-three showing that the resurrection will bring the believer a new body since the old body has been in the state of death (23).

In Gen. 19:24-25, there is the record of God raining fire and brimstone on Sodom and Gomorrah. In verses 27 and 28, it is said that Abraham got up early in the morning and looked toward Sodom and Gomorrah and behold the smoke of those cities going up. This is the twenty-third time the name of Abraham is found.

The twenty-third time the name of Jacob is found, his mother tells him that his brother Esau purposed to kill him (Gen. 27:42).

In Rev. 20:12 says, "I saw the dead, small and great stand before God; and the books were opened." This is the twenty-third time the word "open" is found in Revelation.

NUMBER 24

Twenty-four speaks of the priesthood. In I Chron. 24:1-18, David is said to distribute the priesthood among twenty-four of the descendants of Aaron. After Nadab and Abihu died and left no children, Aaron had two sons left, Eleazer and Ithamar. Among the sons of Eleazer there were sixteen chief men, and of the sons of Ithamar there were eight chief men. Sixteen stands for love and eight the New Birth. To rightly intercede for others, one must have love toward God and must have love toward those for whom he is interceding, and must be truly born again.

In Psalm 72 there are twenty-four things that the Messiah will do for His people. Christ is our High Priest.

NUMBER 40

Forty speaks of trials, testings, and probation. See below how the number "forty" is connected to the testing and probation of Israel.

1. Forty years of probation by trail.
   a. Israel in the wilderness (Deut. 8:2-5).
   b. Israel from crucifixion to destruction of Jerusalem.
2. Forty years of probation by prosperity in deliverance and rest.
   a. Under Othniel (Judg. 3:11).
   b. Under Barak (Judg. 5:31).
   c. Under Gideon (Judg. 8:28).
3. Forty years of probation by prosperity in enlarged dominion.
   a. Under David (II Sam. 5:4).
   b. Under Solomon (I Kings 11:42).
   c. Under Jereboam II (II Kings 12:17-18, 13:3, 5, 22, 25).
   d. Under Joshua (II Kings 12:1).
   e. Under Joash (II Chron. 24:1).
4. Forty years probation by humiliation and servitude.
   a. Israel under the Philistines (Judg. 13:1).

   b. Israel in the time of Eli (I Sam 4:18).
   c. Israel under Saul (Acts 13:21).
5. Forty years probation by waiting.
   a. Moses in Egypt (Acts 7:23).
   b. Moses in Midian (Acts 7:30).

There are seven great periods of testings revealed in the Word of God.

1. Moses was in the mountain of Sinai forty days receiving the law (Ex. 24:18). While he was gone, Israel failed the test (Ex. 32:1).
2. Israel was tried forty years in the wilderness (Num. 14:34).
3. Forty days Elijah spent in Horeb after his experience on Mt. Carmel (I Kings 19:8).
4. Forty days Jonah preached judgment would come to Ninevah (Jonah 3:4).
5. Forty days Ezekiel laid on his right side to symbolize the forty years of Judah's transgression (Ezek. 4:6).
6. Jesus was tempted forty days and nights of the devil (Luke 4:1-2).
7. Forty days Jesus was seen of His disciples, speaking of the things pertaining to the Kingdom of God (Acts 1:3).

NUMBER 50

Fifty represents the Holy Spirit. The Holy Spirit was poured out on the day of Pentecost, which was fifty days after the resurrection of Christ. Jesus said the Holy Spirit would not come until He returned to the Father to act as our High Priest, and as He placed His Blood (30) on the altar for the atonement (20) for our sins, the Holy Spirit (50) would come to bring comfort to the believer.

NUMBER 70

Seventy speaks of Israel and her restoration. The number of descendants of Shem, Ham and Japheth, who populated the Earth after the flood were seventy (Gen. 10).

Seventy persons of Israel's seed came down into Egypt at Joseph's request (Gen. 46:27, Ex. 1:5). Joseph was of the house of Jacob, and came into Egypt from Canaan. Adding him, his two sons and Jacob his father to the sixty-six out of Jacob's loins (Gen. 46:26, 27) accounts for the seventy of the house of Jacob. God used this group to form the Nation Israel.

For seventy years Israel lived in exile and then was restored unto her land (Jer. 25:11; 29:10).

NUMBER 100

One hundred represents God's election of grace - children of promise. Isaac, a child of promise, was born when his father was 100 years old (Gen. 21:5).

The number 100 is connected with Isaac's sowing and reaping, and God's blessing (Gen. 26:12).

Jesus likens those whom He would save unto a Hundred sheep gathered into a fold (Matt. 18:11-12).

There were 100 sockets of silver in the Tabernacle, which were made of 100 talents of silver. Silver was the money given in Redemption (Ex. 30:12-14). Therefore this symbolizes God's election of Grace (Redemption).

NUMBER 144

One hundred forty-four is the Spirit-guided life. This number is the square of twelve, and is naturally associated with Governmental Perfects.

In Rev. Chapter 7, 144,000 were "sealed" by the Holy Spirit of God before God's judgments fall on Earth. This is the number that by the power of the Holy Spirit are kept through the time of trouble.

The children of Israel remained in Egypt 144 years after Joseph's death, and they marched out a free people under the guidance of the Pillar of Fire (a symbol of the presence of God's Spirit).

When Israel was established in the Promised Land, David forms a temple choir (I Chron. 25:7) that consisted of 288 (twice 144), typifying true Spirit-filled praise.

Prophetic Timetable

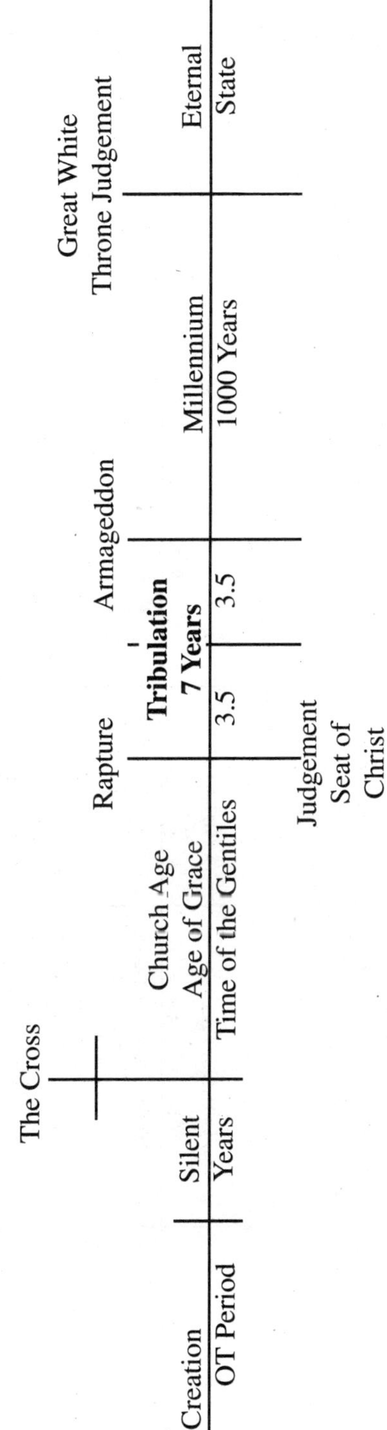

PreMillinnial Timetable

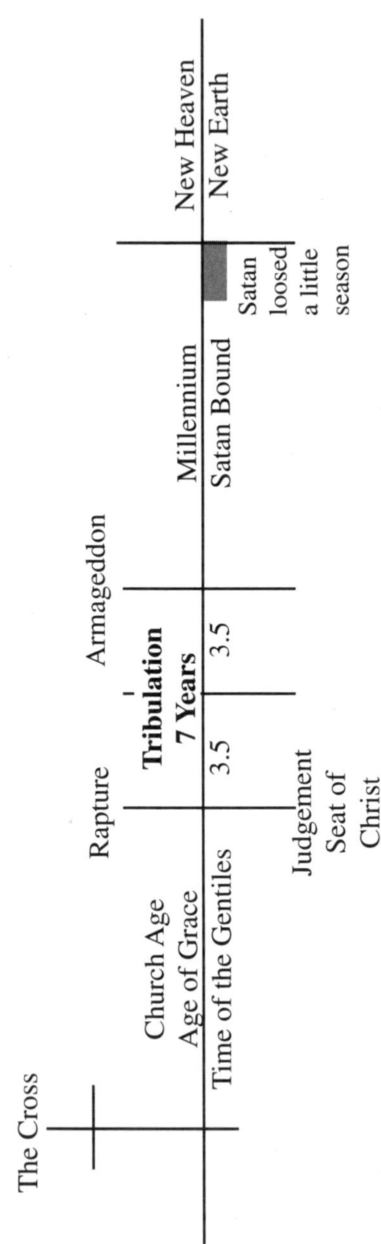

Daniel's Seventy Weeks

Definition: The Seventy weeks of Daniel (or as literally stated in the Hebrew text, "seventy sevens") refer to the time of Jerusalem's desolation under Gentile rule (Dan. 9:2, 12, 16). God revealed to Daniel in answer to prayer that the 70 years of Babylonian Captivity as prophesied by Jeremiah would be extended to "seventy sevens." These "seventy sevens" of years refer to the "Times of the Gentiles" that are determined upon Daniel's people. The reference to Daniel's Seventy Weeks is found in Dan. 9:24-27.

Beginning of the Seventy Weeks: The beginning of the "seventy sevens" was revealed to Daniel (9:25) as being the time of the command or decree to rebuild and to restore the city of Jerusalem (Neh. 1:1-14; 2:1-8). The decree was given in the last of the month Nisan in the 20th year of the reign of Artaxerxes (445 B.C. Neh. 2:1). Other decrees are mentioned in the book of Ezra, but they refer to the rebuilding of the temple and not the city. History places the accession of Artaxerxes at 465 B.C., making his twentieth year 445 B.C. The first of Nisan (Neh. 2:1) is March 1, 445 B.C.

Division of the Seventy Weeks: The beginning of the "seventy sevens" are divided into three sections, namely 7, 62, and 1. The first section of seven sevens and the second section of sixty-two sevens (69 sevens when taken together) end with Messiah's being cut off. The third and last section consisting of only one seven marks a covenant confirmed but broken in the middle of the seven. At the conclusion of the entire seventy-sevens the vision and the prophecy will be fulfilled and everlasting righteousness will be brought in.

End of the Sixty-ninth Seven: The end of the 69th seven marks the cutting off of the Messiah (9:26). This date has been determined by Theologians as approximately April 6, A.D. 32 and is based on Luke 3:1. The public ministry of Jesus Christ began in the 15th year of Tiberias Caesar who began the first year of his reign in A.D. 14 according to the date given by history. From 445 B.C. to A.D. 32 is 476 years, counting 1 B.C. and A.D. 1 as one year. These 476 years mark the duration of the 69 weeks beginning with the decree of Artaxerxes in 445 B.C. to rebuild Jerusalem up to the time when Jesus Christ is cut off in A.D. 32. From this it becomes evident that each seven is equal to one seven-year period.

In order to demonstrate the accuracy of these figures and to demonstrate the accuracy of Bible prophecy, attention has been called to the fact that Biblical years are made up of 360 days per year instead of 365. This can be seen in the duration of the flood mentioned as being five months in Gen. 7:11 and 8:14, while the same period of time is spoken of as being 150 days in Gen. 7:24 and 8:3. Also, in the book of Revelation, 42 months are identified with 1260 days in Rev. 13:4-7, and Rev. 12:6, 13-14. By multiplying 60x7x360, the figure of 173,888 days is obtained for the duration of the 69 weeks. The same number of days may be arrived at 365 days per year basis. Multiplying 476x365 would result in 173,740 days for the 69 sevens. To this would be necessary to add 116 extra days for leap years and leap centuries, also 24 days from March 14 to April 6, making a grand total of 173,880 days.

The Seventieth Week: The mention of the 70th week of Daniel after the cutting off of the Messiah has given place to the following interpretation. (One must remember that the church age is NOWHERE mentioned in prophecy). The 70th week is still future. This seems clear from the mention of the abomination of desolation (Dan. 9:26), which Christ identified with the end of time and His second coming (Matt. 24:15, 21, 29-30). This also leaves room for the destruction of the city of Jerusalem (Dan. 9:26) which did not take place until A.D. 70. Also, the length of the "time of the end" or the second half of the 70th week is in exact harmony with the time dimensions of the future time of trouble described in the book of Revelation (compare Dan. 12:7 with Rev. 12:14 and Rev. 13:5). The 70th week will begin with the great world political leader of the end time making a covenant with Daniel's people, Israel. That the covenant many involve the "daily sacrifice" may be inferred from its mention when the covenant is broken in the middle of the time. The breaking of the covenant in the middle of the time and the creation of the abomination of desolation will mark the beginning of the time of the end, a time of great and unparalleled tribulation in world history just before the battle of Armageddon and the setting up of the Millennial reign of Jesus Christ. The close of the 70th week will mark the introduction of the blessings mentioned in Dan. 9:24.

Will the Church Go through the Tribulation?

I. If the church is in the Tribulation, the Bible would be very plain on such a mighty matter. There is no such definite Scripture in the Bible. A prominent Post-Tribulationalists says, "The author will grant that the Scripture nowhere explicitly states the church will go through the Great Tribulation."

II. Some Scripture to prove Pretribulational Rapture.
Luke 21:35-36 - Note the statement "all these Things." the word escape in Greek is (*ekfeugo*). This word is never used except in a sense of complete removal out of a state or place. Acts 16:27 "been fled" same word as "escape") (Rom. 2:3; II Cor. 11:33; I Thes. 5:3; Heb. 2:3; Heb. 12:25). Never once does it mean "preserved in."
Rev. 3:10 - This is a promise to take the churches "out from" the hour of temptation (tribulation). Note four things:

1. The language of this promise goes beyond local persecution. It corresponds to other language given elsewhere of the great tribulation.
2. Much Scripture has a "double reference" -This one does.
3. The promise is given to all the churches (v. 13).
4. Verses preceding and following refer to second coming. At the end of chapter 3, the word "church" disappears until chapter 19. Chapter 18 in Revelation ends the Great Tribulation, then the word "church" is mentioned (Rev. 19:6-9). At this time the church is seen in Heaven, not on Earth.

III. The Rapture described.
I Thes. 4:13-18
Matt. 24:36-42 - Comparison of time and conditions before the flood with time and conditions before the rapture.

Took = To take away by destroying
Taken = (*paralambano*) - To take home or receive.
(Matt. 1:20; John 14:3)

John 14:1-3 - "Let not your heart be troubled" - would be if we knew we would go through the Tribulation.

Revelation Chapter One

1:1

This verse introduces immediately the theme of the book, namely, Jesus Christ in His present and future glory. The prophetic nature of the book is revealed in the words "A revelation of Jesus Christ." Revelation (*apokalypsis*) meaning "disclosure, or unveiling." It is a revelation of truth about Christ — His coming when He will be revealed. It is also a revelation from Christ. The word "revelation" occurs eighteen times in the New Testament (Gal. 1:12; II Thes. 1:7; I Peter 1:7, 13; 4:13, etc.). This is not a closed book, but a revealed book.

Jesus Christ received His kingdom from God (Luke 19:15) and shall deliver it up to God (I Cor. 15:24). The purpose is "to show" and not to hide.

"Things" used 45 times in Revelation.

1. Events of the whole church age.
2. Events in Heaven.
3. Events of the Tribulation (Daniel's 70th week).
4. Events of the Millennial Reign.
5. Events of the eternal new Heaven and new Earth.

These things "must" (absolute certainty) come to pass.

Shortly (*tachos*) - indicates swiftness of action. It doesn't mean that the things would all come to pass in John's day, but that when it starts, there will be a rapid succession of events.

Signified (*semaino*) - To make a clear record by signs and symbols.

1:2

John gives three things that reveal the authenticity of the writings of Revelation:

1. He wrote down on parchment the Word of God.
2. Jesus' words as He spoke to John.
3. The eye-witnessing of what he wrote about.

1:3

This is the only book that promises a blessing to the reader. Look at what the blessing is contingent upon:

1. Those that read —
2. With the intention of hearing what he reads —
3. And with the intention of keeping (retaining as truth) the things heard.

There are seven "beatitudes" in Revelation:

1. The Blessed Challenge (1:3)
2. The Blessed Comfort (14:13)
3. The Blessed Cautiousness (16:15)
4. The Blessed Calling (19:9)
5. The Blessed Conquest (20:6)
6. The Blessed Cherishing (22:7)
7. The Blessed Conformity (22:14)

"Prophecy" used seven times in Revelation.

"The time is at hand" — Time (*kairos* = proper time/occasion) = Space of time or chronology. It has no limits such as "short" or "long." When John wrote Revelation, the church age had already come. John was saying the contents of Revelation were the next things to come to pass in chronological order of God's plan, regardless of when it came.

1:4

"To the seven churches" - There were other churches not mentioned here (Colossae-Col. 1:2) (Troas - II Cor. 2:12) (Miletus - Acts 20:17) (Hierapolis - Col. 4:12). Why did John single out seven churches?

1. These churches are centers of seven political districts.
2. These churches are representative of typical churches down through the centuries until the church shall be removed.
3. There are only seven basic types of churches in every generation until Jesus comes. These letters are measuring-

lines by which all churches can measure themselves in the light of the Lord Jesus.

"From Him which is" - Referring to God (Ex. 3:14 - The "self existing one"). The statement in Greek is: "From He which is." In Greek as in English, when a noun is governed by a preposition it changes its case. But John refuses to change it. Why? John was showing such immense reverence for God that he refuses to alter the name for God, even when the rules of grammar demand alteration. Literally, "from the He is; from the He was; and from the He is for all time to come."

"The seven spirits" = Refers to sevenfold virtues of the Holy Spirit (Isa. 11:2).

1:5

Verses 5 & 6 of Revelation One call those who do not believe in the Trinity a liar!

In verse 5 our Lord is called "the faithful witness," reminding us of His earthly life. The word "witness" comes from the Greek word *martus* which means martyr.

"The first begotten from the dead" refers to His resurrection (I Cor. 15:20-23). "First begotten" refers to supremacy or pre-eminent dignity and not to time or chronological sequence (Psa. 89:27).

As the "prince of the kings of the Earth," Christ has the power to reign and rule.

There are three major things Jesus had done for us.

1. He loved us (Eph. 3:17-19) - Present tense—continuous.
2. He washed us from our sin in His own blood. WASH (*louein*) = To loose or release. Aorist tense - An act completed and finished in the past-not have been done again.
3. He made us kings and priests unto God (I Pet. 2:9). We will reign in Christ's kingdom (Dan. 7:13-14, Luke 1:32-33) and we shall serve Christ as a priest - giving us total access to God.

1:7

The Second Advent of Jesus is a vital part of our Christian testimony. But, it is essential to distinguish between the two distinctive parts into which the Coming divides.

1. There are many Scriptures that refer to the coming of the Lord for His saints: John 14:3; Phil. 3:20; I Thes. 4:15-17; I Cor. 15:23. This is the Rapture.
2. There is another set of Scriptures that teach that Jesus will come with the saints (Jude 14; Zech. 14:5; Col. 3:4, Rev. 19:11-14). These are references to the glorious appearing of our Lord who comes back to the Earth after the Tribulation to break the manifested power of evil on Earth. Rev. 1:7 refers to this coming with the saints.

Dan. 7:1-14 has a vision of four bestial powers who held the world in their grip. But, in Dan. 7:13-14 the day of these bestial and savage empires was over, and the power was given to "one like the son of man."

"Every eye shall see Him" must be accepted literally. There is one class singled out from the mass of mankind, namely, "they that pierced Him." John is quoting Zech. 12:10. There will come a day when all who have "crucified Christ" and refused to trust Him as Savior will find Him as Judge and will fall in worship before Him - but too late.

"Even So, amen" - (*nai-amen*) - Yes indeed, so let it be.

1:8

The announcement of these divine titles forms a fitting conclusion to the introduction. Here God is announcing His own titles through Christ. He is the eternal "I am," a verb indicating "being" but not "becoming." Christ was before time began; He is now; and He will be when time ends.

1:9

Here John introduces himself. John gives his right to speak as "one who has been a companion in trouble." John puts three words together here: tribulation, kingdom, patience.

> Tribulation (*thlipsis*) - Not word for Great Tribulation. It means literally: "The pressure of a rock." John is referring to persecution already befallen the believers (II Tim. 3:12).

Kingdom (*Basileia*) - Referring to the present state of the kingdom (John 3:3). This is not the millennial kingdom.

Patience (*hupomone*) - Steadfast endurance. This all-conquering endurance is the one thing that can turn affliction into glory. This is done by Jesus Christ and not in our own energy.

Patmos is a barren rocky little island about ten miles long by five miles wide. It is about 800 feet high and barren of trees. It lies forty miles off the coast of Asia Minor. Paul was banished to the island as a common form of Roman punishment.

He was banished because of "the Word of God and for the testimony of Jesus Christ."

1:10

"In the Spirit" - John was controlled by an absolute subservience to the Spirit. He found himself in another state of being (Ezek. 3:12). The voice John heard was like the sound of a trumpet. This language is woven into the New Testament (Matt. 24:31; I Cor. 15:42; I Thes. 4:16).

The entire content of his book of Revelation was communicated in a vision "on the Lord's Day." This is a reference to the first day of the week (Lev. 23:15 - Acts 2).

1:11

Here the Lord commands to "write in a book" the things John is about to see. The order of listing the churches is no accident since it represents the seven divisions of Church History from Christ until the present.

1:12

John turned to identify whose voice it was that was talking to him. When he turned, he saw "seven golden candlesticks."

Candlesticks (*luchnia*) - Better translated "lampstands." A candle consumes itself while burning and a lamp burns from oil that feeds the wick. Oil is symbolic of the Holy Spirit. He is not referring to the "light" but the "holders of the light." These are seven different lampstands standing on their own base, referring to the independent assemblies of churches.

Christ does for the church today what Aaron did for the lamps in the Tabernacle (Ex. 3:7-8; 37:23; 40:25).

1:13

Christ is pictured standing in the midst of the "lampstands" (churches). That's where He wants to be. Everything should revolve around Christ (Dan. 7:13). "The son of man" refers to Jesus Christ.

The word "garment" is robe (*poderas*) which means, "reaching down to the feet." There are three pictures given in the Bible concerning this robe:

1. The Old Testament uses this word to describe the robe of the High Priest (Ex. 28:4; 29:5; Lev. 16:4). At present Jesus is carrying on His priestly work as our high priest in the presence of God.
2. This robe was also the attire of princes and kings (I Sam. 18:24; 24:5, 12; Ezek. 26:16). Jesus is wearing the robe of royalty. He is now king.
3. This is also the dress of the Messenger of God (Dan. 10:5). Here Jesus is shown as the supreme Messenger of God.

Here we see Jesus girt about the breast (not the loins, as usual) with a golden girdle. Gold here sets forth divine righteousness. Girt about the breast indicates divine judgment. The angels of judgment in Rev. 15:6 wore the same kind of garment.

1:14

The next three verses give a series of descriptions of the Risen Christ.

"His head and His hair" - white like wool and snow (Dan. 7:9). Speaks of two things:

1. It stands for the great age, thus illustrating the eternal existence of Jesus.
2. It stands for divine purity.

"His eyes as a flame of fire" (Dan. 10:6). This speaks of His omniscience - His "all-seeing" - "all-knowing."

1:15
"His feet were like fine brass." This stands for strength and the immovable steadfastness of God.

"His voice as the sound of many waters" (Ezek. 43:2). This is the voice of judgment and power and authority (Matt. 25:41; Jer. 25:30).

1:16
"In His right hand seven stars." We are told in verse 20 that the seven stars represent the "Angels of the seven churches." The "right hand" betokens supreme authority and power and honor (Psa. 110:1; Eph. 1:20; Rev. 5:1, 7). "Out of His mouth went a sharp two-edged sword." This represents the penetrating quality of the Word of God (Heb. 4:12; I Sam. 49:2). The Battle of Armageddon will be won by a Word (Rev. 19:15).

"His Countenance was as the sun shineth in His strength." (Matt. 17:2). This represents the glowing glory of Jesus Christ (Judg. 5:4).

1:17
The effect of the glorious vision of Christ was overpowering. To be in His presence is always overpowering (Isa. 6:1-7; Ezek. 1:28; Dan. 8:17-18; 10: 7-10). The Lord also put His "Hand of Power" on the Lord.

1:18
The great truth of the death and resurrection is here confirmed by Jesus Christ. How glorious it is to know that Jesus Christ has the power over the grave because of His own overcoming death. Jesus Christ also has the keys to Hell. Really, He is the key.

1:19
This passage gives the key to Revelation. This is the only book in the Bible where the outline is recorded by the Lord.

1. "The things which thou has seen." This is Rev. 1:12-16 (see verses 12 and 17).
2. "The things which are." Rev. chapters 2 and 3. the Seven Churches.
3. "The things which shall be hereafter." (Literally - *meta - tauta*)

After these things, immediately following. Actually saying "the things which shall be after the church periods ends." Rev. Chapters 4-22.

1:20

"Angels" can be better translated "Ministers of Christ." This represents any person of spiritual leadership whom God sets in the Church as the leading minister. Christ Himself is the authority and head of the church. It is the business of the minister to "shine as stars" and keep in his appointed course!

Revelation Chapter Two

It is worthy to note that the message to the Seven Churches in chapters two and three comes between two visions, the Vision of Christ in the midst of the seven candlesticks in chapter one and the Vision of the Four and Twenty Elders round about the throne in chapter four. We shall now learn something about each candlestick (church) and how it applies to the present and future age of the church.

There are three points concerning these seven churches which are extremely important in the interpretation of the Scriptures:

1. These churches were actual historical churches in the province of Asia Minor in the closing decade of the first century.
2. These churches are representative churches. Individually or collectively they represent conditions and circumstances in all the churches in all the world from the beginning of the church in Christ's day to the end of the church age at the Rapture.
3. These churches are also prophetic. These churches are given in Scripture just as the seven divisions of the church age have occurred from the Cross of Calvary to the Crown of Glory.

Another fact our Lord does not speak of concerning these churches of Asia is the "one-church" idea. They were not federated into one corporation or body. Each was distinct, autonomous and sovereign. The true church of the Lord will have NO part in a "world church" idea, but will remain an autonomous, sovereign and distinct congregation.

As we consider the significance of these seven churches as a whole, let us note that each church yields to the same seven fold outline.

1. The Christ is described in each letter.
2. The Commendation which is given in praise of the virtues and victories of the church.
3. The Criticism is offered. Wherever there is evil it is exposed and rebuked.

4. The Call is heard. A call to repentance, to return to the true faith and to faithful service and consistent living above all worldliness.
5. The Characteristics are mentioned. That which is peculiar to each church is revealed.
6. The Crown is offered or the reward for those who will heed the promptings of the Spirit and hold fast and be faithful to the Christ.
7. The Comprehension is revealed, by this we mean each church points to a certain period of time in the history of this age.

I. Ephesus: The Backslidden Church. (Rev. 2:1-7) The Apostolic Church - A.D. 30-A.D. 100

Ephesus was the chief city of the province of Asia. It was both the religious and commercial center of the area at that time. There are five things about the city of Ephesus we should note:

1. It had a large artificial harbor that could accommodate the largest ships of the world.
2. It was a political free city.
3. It was the center of the worship of Diana of the Ephesians.
4. It was a center of pagan superstition.
5. It was a city of mixed population.

2:1 The Observer

"Angel" should read "messenger," or the leader of the church. "Ephesus" means "desired ones." This was the most desirable church of the church age. The most fervent days of evangelism characterized the ministry of this church. Now we have two descriptions of the Lord: First He is "He who holds the seven stars in His right hand."

"HOLD" (*kratein*) = To have complete control over that which is held. The stars are the Church's light bearers — they derive their light from Him, subject to His power and sustained by Him. (I would not want to be a pastor if I did not have this assurance.)

SECOND: "He walks in the midst of the seven golden candlesticks." The candlesticks or lampstands are the churches. This tells of Christ's unwearied activity in the midst of His churches.

2:2-3 The Occupation

No good thing is overlooked by the Lord. There are six things He acknowledges in the church of Ephesus: work, labor, patience, discipline, bearing of burdens, and courage in activity.

"I KNOW" - God's absolute knowledge of ALL.

"LABOR" (*kopos*) - Stronger word than "work." - To work to the point of exhaustion in mind, strength, time and treasure.

"PATIENCE" (*hupomone*) - Courage that accepts suffering and hardships and loss and turns them into grace and glory (II Pet. 1:5-6, James 1:2-4).

"CANST NOT BEAR THE EVIL ONES" This shows discipline. If a member was living in double life, he was not tolerated. This church was more interested in quality of members than quantity.

"TRIED—AND FOUND LIARS." They also disciplined the pulpit. They would not bear those who were pretenders. They were to be tested as to their validity.

"HAST BOURN—HAST NOT FAINTED." Here was a church that also was willing to bear reproach for Christ's sake. They were not ashamed of Christ's cause or of Christ. It was a virile, vital, vigorous church. There was never a thought of giving up.

2:4 The Offense

In all their zeal for orthodoxy, something had gone wrong. They had left their first love.

What is "First Love?" It is simply "Loving Jesus first." The man who allows his first fervent love for His Savior to grow lukewarm is a backslider. And, it isn't just "a word of mouth." Do we love Jesus first? Before TV on Sunday night etc. What is our first love? (What about a couple at their wedding day?)

2:5 The Obligation

The Lord gives three steps that must be followed if they are to return to a right relationship with Him.

1. "Remember" - Call to mind these early days when the first named fruit of the Spirit flooded your soul (Rom. 5:5, Gal. 5:22).

2. "Repent" - Repentance is the admission that the fault is ours, and the experience of a Godly sorrow that it is so."

3. "Return" - No man has truly repented when he continues to do the same thing over and over again.

Then He gives a warning - "I will remove thy candlestick out of his place." Their testimony would be taken from them. (The church in Ephesus has been gone for centuries).

2:6 The Orthodoxy

Here we meet a heresy the Lord says He hates, and He praises Ephesus for also hating this heresy. This was "the deeds of the Nicolaitanes." This heresy was coming from within the church - "This thou hast."

These Nicolaitanes doctrine was basically threefold:

1. The law is ended; therefore, there are no laws or rules and regulations, and we are entitled to do what we like (see Gal. 5:13).
2. They argued that the body is evil anyway, and that the spirit alone is good. Therefore, a man could do what he liked with his body because the body didn't matter.
3. They argued that the Christian was so defended by grace that he could go anywhere and do anything and take no harm.

2:7 The Overcomer

Here Christ is trying to alert the dull of ears (Matt. 11:15).

Who is the overcomer? The truly born again - one who has been redeemed through faith in Christ. Jesus is the overcomer, and we are overcomers by virtue of our position in Him (John 16:33; I John 5:4-5). The day we trusted the Lord is the day we became an overcomer (I John 4:4)! We are already overcomers, but so many won't take what's theirs.

"The Tree of Life." To the overcomer is promised by the Lord, they shall have the privilege of "eating of the fruits" of the Tree of Life (Rev. 22:2). This means we will have perfect health and a perfect life forever.

II. Smyrna: The Commended Church

Of all the cities of Asia, Smyrna was the loveliest. It was located north of Ephesus about 50 miles on the Aegean Sea. Smyrna was one of the few planned cities in the world. In 600 B.C. the Lydians destroyed the city. About 200 B.C. Lysimachus rebuilt Smyrna as a planned city.

Here we have an interesting thing which shows the real significance of the inspiration of Scripture. The Living Lord is called "He who was dead and is alive again." This phrase was an echo of the experience of Smyrna itself.

Smyrna represents the Persecuted Church of church history from A.D. 100 to A.D. 312.

The word "Smyrna" is the Greek word *smyrna.* It is the word from which we get our word "myrrh", and means "bitter". Myrrh only gives out its fragrance when its leaves are crushed, so the sweet fragrance ascended to God during this period.

There is not one word of censure in this letter to Smyrna. It is all praise.

2:8 The Conquering Christ

Jesus wanted this poverty-stricken, suffering church to know that, regardless of what was happening, He was still on the scene and must be still first in their lives. His authority rested upon His death and resurrection—"Dead and alive".

2:9 The Crushing Conditions

Here is trilogy that produced deep spirituality.

TRIBULATION (*thlipsis*) — A grinding, heavy millstone that grinds wheat into flour by its weight. Here it is the pressure of persecution, sorrow and death.

POVERTY — There are two words in Greek for poverty:

1. *Penia* - A man who works for a living and barely makes it.

2. *Ptocheia* - Absolute and utter destitution-beggary.

The second word is the one used here. But, they were rich in salvation, in their knowledge of God, in their faith, in their fellowship one with another, and in their heavenly communion with God. Rich is *plousios* from which we get our word "PLUTOCRAT". We are God's "plutocrats".

"BLASPHEMY" here means "slander". These slanderous liars are said to be really "Satan-worshippers" - or from the very headquarters of the devil.

2:10A The Courage in Conflict

Jesus said to them "Fear none of these things". The Christian must ever look beyond grief to glory.

We are told that some of them would be cast into prison by the devil's influence that they might be tried. (Satan in behind all trouble today—although God may permit it.)

"Ten Days" - Why is this expression given? Ten is the earthly number for "testimony". The world will do everything possible to destroy the testimony of the saints. The real significance is that the Lord was telling them that it would cost them something to be a Christian.

2:10B The Crusader's Crown

This is an admonishment to faithfulness in martyrdom for the saints. It is "unto death" not "until death". They were not to recant in the fore of a martyr's death.

"FAITHFUL" - To be convinced. Rev. 1:5 says Jesus is the "faithful *martus* (witness) or martyr. What Jesus was saying was not "keep your chin up" or "keep smiling" or "the power of positive thinking", but to be "convinced" of Him and let Him be their strength and courage.

"A Crown of Life" (James 1:12). CROWN is *stephanos*. There are two words for "crown" in Greek.

1. *diadema*: A Royal Crown

2. *stephanos*: A Victor's Crown

Here it is the crown of joy and victory offered to the faithful witness.

There are five crowns mentioned in the New Testament:

1. The Incorruptible Crown (I Cor. 9:25) given to the one who faithfully runs the race of life.
2. The Crown of Rejoicing (I Thes. 2:19) given to the soul winner.
3. The Crown of Righteousness (II Tim. 4:8) given to those who love His appearing and who have a holy walk on Earth.
4. The Crown of Glory (I Pet. 5:4) for the shepherd (pastor) who faithfully teaches the Word.
5. The Crown of Life (Rev. 2:10; James 1:12) for those who suffer for Christ.

2:11 The Comforting Conversation

"He that hath an ear" — brings it to individual responsibility of the believer to HEAR (to listen with an attitude to respond). The "overcomer" is the true believer as we have already seen. "The Second Death" is something the Christian can have no part in Rev. 20:6. The "first death" is the separation of spirit and body (James 2:26).

III. Pergamos: "Dwelling where Satan's throng is." Represents A.D. 312-606.

Satan found that he could not destroy the church by making martyrs of men. That but increased their loyalty to Christ. So now he tries a new tactic, that of introducing the world into the church.

Pergamos was located about sixty miles northeast of Smyrna. At this time Pergamos was called "the most famous city" in the world. It was a center of culture. Pergamos had a library that contained no fewer than 200,000 parchment rolls. It was in Pergamos that parchment was invented. Parchment was made from the skins of beasts, tanned, smoothed and polished and prepared for writing.

Pergamos was also a great center of heathen religions. It had a shrine erected to the god of Zeus. It was built in front of the Temple of Athene which stood 800 feet up on Pergamum's conical hill. It was forty feet high and it stood on a projecting ledge of a rock. It looked exactly like a great throne on the hillside and all day every day it smoked with the smoke of sacrifices offered to Zeus. It has been suggested that the great altar was "Satan's seat."

Pergamos was also famous for its Temple to Aesculopius. He was the god of healing, who was worshipped under the symbol of a serpent. Here was located one of the greatest medical schools in the world.

The etymology of the word *pergamos* is "marriage." Constantine, when he became emperor of Rome in A.D. 312, by imperial decree, lifted the ban against Christians. He declared that the religion of the Roman Empire must be Christianity, and compelled all the armies to be baptized; thereby uniting (marrying) church and state.

2:12 The Sovereign with the Sword

This salutation speaks of judgment by the Word of God. Pergamos was catering to wicked men and would have to face the sword of the Word which proceeds out of the mouth of Him who dictated this letter (Heb. 4:12).

2:13 The Service and the Suffering

The church was in a difficult position. The Christians in Pergamos are living in the very headquarters of Satan. During this period the doctrine of Arius came into the church. It is known today as Unitarianism. Arius preached that Christ was not the eternal Son of God. He declared that he was merely another created being. In my opinion, his creed is what "Jehovah's Witnesses" and other cults teach. But this church remained true to the Deity of Christ.

These people were faithful to the name of Jesus to the point that Antipas was martyred because of his stand. Jesus gives Antipas a title that He had (Rev. 1:5) - "Witness" is *martus* which means martyr.

2:14-15 The Stumbling and the Sin

In spite of the fidelity of the Church at Pergamos, there is error there. The church had tolerated those in their midst who were Balaamites and Nicolaitanes.

The history of Balaam is given in Num. 22-25. He was an hireling prophet used by a wicked king. Read his nauseating story in Numbers 22-25. The "stumbling block before Israel" was the offering of the hospitality of his kingdom to Israel in which Israel became mixed up with heathenism. The "eating of things sacrificed unto idols" was a cheapening of sacred things. "Fornication" had a twofold meaning: (1) Spiritual fornication and (2) literal fornication as an act of worship.

In the church at Ephesus, the "deeds of the Nicolaitanes" are mentioned. Here the "doctrine of the Nicolaitanes" is mentioned. It was between A.D. 400-600 that the "deeds" became "doctrines." Nicolaitanism is the doctrine of a strong ecclesiastical hierarchy (clergy) ruling over the laity. Note that the Lord "hates" this. A partial list of changes that took place in the church under Nicolaitanism follows:

A.D. 320 - Prayers for the dead.
A.D. 375 - Worship of saints and angels.
A.D. 394 - Mass was first instituted.
A.D. 416 - Baptism by sprinkling introduced.
A.D. 431 - Worship of Mary begun.
A.D. 500 - Priests began dressing different from laymen.
A.D. 519 - Easter and lent observances introduced.
A.D. 593 - The doctrine of purgatory introduced.
A.D. 600 - Worship services conducted in Latin.

2:16 The Safety and the Severe Sentence

Repent (*metano-eson*) - Change your mind. The "coming quickly" is a lack of hesitation to punish the church for permitting such in its midst. He here refers to the judging power of His Word. His wrath to "fight against them" is directed against those who were deceiving the church. The Lord's wrath is always hottest against those who lead others astray.

2:17a The Statement of the Spirit

Here again the Lord commands His people to give heed to the voice of the Spirit. It is the duty of the Holy Spirit in the churches to magnify and glorify Jesus. If we will hear and heed the voice of the Spirit, blessings will follow.

2:17b The Supper and the Stone

The "overcomer" here is (as elsewhere) the personal relationship with Jesus Christ. To this person He gives three promises:

1. "Give to eat of the hidden manna." *Manna* means "What is this?" For 12,500 mornings Jehovah rained down "manna" upon the camp of Is-

rael. It was not "hidden" because the people gathered it every day. Manna is a type of Jesus Christ (John 6:30-31; John 6:48 -56). The trials which had beset the Christians at Pergamos were difficult. They were called upon to bear witness for Christ in the very headquarters of Satan. How did they do it? They partook daily of Christ. He was hidden from the view of those who rejected Him.

2. The white stone was employed in the social life and judicial customs of the ancients. Days of festivity were known by a white stone-days of calamity by a black stone. A white stone meant acquittal - a black stone meant condemnation in the courts. This means that the Christian acquitted, justified in the sight of God, because of Jesus Christ.

3. The "new name" refers to Christ. It is because of Him that we are declared "not guilty" (Rom. 5:1).

IV. Thyatira (2:18-29)

"The Pagan Church" (A.D. 606-A.D. 1520)

2:18 "The Son is the Judge"

It is significant indeed that the speaker here refers to Himself as the "Son of God." Perhaps the severity of the rebuke contemplated here made proper that a more impressive reference to the authority of the speaker be given.

The description of the Son of God here is part of the description given in Rev. 1:14-15 (Dan. 10:6). These eyes represent the awful penetration of the gaze that strips the disguise away and sees into a man's inmost heart.

The "feet of brass" represent the swift feet of judgment that belong to Jesus Christ.

2:19 The Service of the Just

Although the church as a whole was "rotten to the core," there were many true believers who had a personal love for Christ that was manifested in their works. Here are six words of commendation given to them:

"WORKS" - This is used twice, indicating that the darker the night, the greater their effort - more numerous, more pure, more elevated in character as the "fruit of faith."

"CHARITY" - This is a word for "love." Love led the list of their virtues. It is the very essence of Divine nature (I John 4:8, 16). Although this church corresponds to the Dark Ages of church history (A.D. 606-1520). There were those - Peter Waldo, John Wycliffe, John Huss, Savanarola and Anslem maintained good works for a great love for truth and the Lord.

"SERVICE" (*Diakonian*) from which we get Deacon. The word means "ministry." It is used here as a collective ministering of a local assembly (Acts 11:29; Rom. 15:26 I Cor. 16:1). These faithful few were meeting the needs of people.

"FAITH" (*Pistos*) = faithfulness or loyalty. These saints were dependable and loyal and reliable. They were not occasional and spasmodic.

"PATIENCE" (*Hupomone*) = To remain under, with endurance and proper mental and emotional balance. Do you have the capacity to "be still" when all around you is storm-tossed?

2:20-21 The Sin of Jezebel

The Lord had a grave indictment against the Thyatiran Church. This church had permitted an evil in its midst of a more serious character than any that had yet appeared. The words of this passage are meaningless unless they are viewed prophetically.

"SUFFERING" - "To allow." This church allowed sin to creep in. It did not judge sin and condemn it.

"THAT WOMAN JEZEBEL" - In this church existed a woman of like character of Jezebel in the Old Testament. She was not a true messenger of divine truth. She had urged the people of Thyatira to continue their pagan worship of idols. II Kings 9:22 gives a rather factual picture of Jezebel.

This woman "called herself" a Prophetess. Her philosophy must have had some truth in it to hold the errors together.

This woman is accused of teaching two things:

1. Teaching the Thyatirans to commit fornication. The question must be answered, "Is this literal sexual immorality or is it spiritual infidelity to God?" In Scripture, spiritual infidelity is often expressed in terms of adultery and fornication (Ex. 34:15-16; Deut. 31:16; Psa. 73:27; Hos. 9:1). I rather believe that the reference here is to infidelity to Jesus Christ.

2. To eat things sacrificed to idols. When made a sacrifice to an idol in a Greek Temple, very little of the actual meat was burned on the altar. The priest received a share of the meat and the worshipper received the rest. Many would take the meat home and hold a feast in his house. Here was the Christians problem. Could a Christian go to one of these feasts and eat the meat that had been offered to idols? The Christian knew where his duty lay (Act. 15:29).

In verse 21 the Lord says He had patiently dealt with this false woman for over a period of time and she had refused to repent.

2:22-25 The Severity of Judgment

The word "bed" here is not usually used for the "harlots bed" but for the "bed of affliction." This Jezebel and all those who have followed her teachings are those to whom the Lord refers.

"Great Tribulation" here is not "The Great Tribulation." It refers to a time of sorrow and judgment and trial that will be sent by the Lord for their spiritual harlotry. Only repentance can avoid these consequences.

Those "children" that come after her will eventually be "killed with death." This finds its answer in Revelation chapters 17 and 18.

The design of this judgment will be so apparent that it will convince all that the Lord knows what is in the heart of man - even to the innermost secrets (reins) of the innermost being (heart).

Then a uniform rule is laid down by which God will judge men. According to their works. This is not a reference to a "giving of salvation" according to works, but to the saved it is a "giving of rewards" according to their works; and to the lost it is a "giving of punishment" according to their works (Rev. 20:12-13; Rom. 14:10; II Cor. 5:10).

"Unto the rest in Thyatira" seems to indicate that even this terrible system has a remnant of saved people. The Lord here promises not to add any further burden of truth to them. He encouraged them to "hold fast" and not surrender their firm convictions.

2:26-29 The Saints and Their Joys

In verses 26-27 the chaplet of victory is placed on the brow of the one who perseveres in the path of faithfulness to the end. Here Jesus' works are contrasted to the works of Jezebel (v. 23).

The promise here is directly connected with the second Psalm (Psa. 2:8-9). The promise to the overcomer assures him that he is to share with Christ in His judgment administrations over the nations (Jude 14-15; Matt. 19:28; I Cor. 6:2; I Cor. 6:3). In verse 28 the star is Christ Himself (Rev. 22:16; Num. 24:17; II Peter 1:19).

Revelation Chapter Three

V. Sardis - Failure to Live the Name

"The Dead Church" - A.D. 1520 -A.D. 1750

You will note that Christ has NO word on commendation for this church at Sardis. He addresses a word of commendation to a few individuals of the church, but not to the church itself.

Sardis stood in the plain of the valley of the river Hermus. It was situated about 50 miles east of Smyrna and 30 miles southeast of Thyatira. It was an important and wealthy city located on the commercial trade route running east and west through Lydia.

The wealth of Sardis was legendary. There, money was invented. The first gold and silver coins ever minted were the work of Croesus in the capital city of Sardis.

When John wrote his letter to Sardis, Sardis was a degenerate church in a degenerate city.

The people of Sardis were idolaters - they worshipped the mother goddess Cyhele (Mother of gods). Her worship was of the most debasing character, and orgies of the foulest and darkest impurity were committed on the occasions.

The church at Sardis was called a "dead church" though it had a name to live. It had a "form of godliness without the power."

The word Sardis means "ones who come out" or "remnant." This makes it clear that the Reformation period of A.D. 1520-1750 is reached in the letter to Sardis.

3:1 Christ Comprehending Their Condition

"The seven spirits of God" is a presentation of Christ who imparts the fullness of the spirit to the church. Only through the operation of the Holy Spirit can a dead church be made alive. The plenitude of the Spirit is given in Isa. 11:2 - the unity of the Spirit is given in Eph. 4:3-6. Wherever sin and failure mark a local assembly, one can be certain the Holy Spirit has not been in command of the hearts of the people. You will remember that the "stars" represent the churches and their pastors.

The terrible accusation against the church of Sardis is that, although it has a reputation for life, it is, in fact, spiritually dead. The world may say "there is a live church," but the Lord may say, "Thou art dead." It must have been a beehive of organized activity. There was nothing lacking in the outward appearance of this church. But the Lord said it was dead.

3:2-3 Christ Commends Their Consecration

If anything is to be rescued from the impending ruin of the Church in Sardis, the necessity is that the Christians should awaken and be on the "watch." Watchfulness should be the constant attitude of the Christian life (I Cor. 16:13; I Pet. 5:8). What little they still had of spiritual things was ready to die.

The word "perfect" literally means "finished" or "complete." They were not carrying out God's purpose for their existence. The church was living a lie. When the Great Physician felt their spiritual pulse, He pronounced them dead! Do we know the difference between appearance and reality (Isa. 29:13)?

Verse 3 relates that self-judgment is always preferable to being judged by the Lord (I Cor. 11:31). The word "remember" is the present imperative, and it means "keep on remembering." Christ is telling the church to remember the enthusiasm and the thrill with which they first heard the message of the gospel.

The word "repent" is an aorist imperative which describes one definite action. There must come a decisive moment when a person decides to be done with the old way.

"Hold Fast" is also a present imperative - Never stop keeping the tenets of the gospel. This is a warning against spasmodic Christianity.

The Lord promises this church that if they do not repent of their sins, He would come upon them as a thief (without their even noticing it), and without any display of action, their candlestick would be complete removed. When this happens, a church is finished!

3:4 Christ Compliments the Constancy

Again Christ speaks to a faithful remnant found in the mass of dead formalism. There were a few people who had not "defiled their garments."

The word "few" (*oligos*) means "slight" or "little." These people were a very small minority.

The word "garments" is used figuratively here. What clothes are to the flesh, so habits and actions are to the real self. So, the Christian should exercise care about the wardrobe of the soul (Col. 3:8, 12-14).

They had washed their robes and made them white in the blood of the Lamb, and would therefore walk with the glorified Savior in white robes. "They are worthy" could be made only about persons washed in the blood - saved by God's grace.

3:5-6 Christ - The Clothing and the Confession

The overcomer (truly "born-again" ones) will be clothed in white raiment (Rev. 19:8; Zech. 3:1-8).

The "Book of Life" is the register of all who ever lived. It is God's record of the names of men. Every person at one time has his name in that book.

Those whose names are erased are those who never became saved! Moses was familiar with this fact (Ex. 32:32). To be blotted out means eternal death (Rev. 20:15). To preserve your name in the Book of Life by trusting Jesus is of the highest importance (Luke 10:20; Dan. 12:1).

Here again the promise of Matt. 10:32, 33 is made. A promise to "confess before the Father" all who will confess Him as Savior.

VI. Philadelphia - The God-honoring Church

A.D. 1750-A.D. 1900

The message to the church at Philadelphia is in some respect one of the most interesting of all the messages to the churches. Philadelphia was the youngest of all the seven churches. Here is a church which was faithful to Christ and the word of God.

The name "Philadelphia" literally means "brotherly love." This church represents the period of A.D. 1750-A.D. 1900. This age is called the "period of Modern Missions." Love is the mainspring of all Christian service (II Cor. 5:14; John 14:23).

3:7-8 The Deity and the Door

"He that is Holy" - This is also a description of God Himself (Isa. 6:3; 43:15). Now this title is given to the risen Christ. Holy (Hagios) means "different - separate from."

"He that is true" - There are two words for "true" in Greek.

1. *Alethes* - true in the sense that it is different from "false."

2. *Alethinos* - means real or genuine, not an imitation quality. In Jesus there is reality (John 1:9; 14:6; 15:1; I John 5:20).

"He that hath the Key of David." This is a reference to the authority of Christ (Luke 1:32:33).

"He that openeth, and no man shutteth, and shutteth, and no man openeth." The doors of opportunity for preaching the gospel are controlled by the Lord Jesus Christ. The Lord is presented as the doorkeeper to opportunity. The greatest days of missionary opportunity in the history of the church was A.D. 1750-A.D. 1900.

"I have set before thee an open door, and no man can shut it!" This is the door of missionary opportunity and witnessing (I Cor. 16:9; II Cor. 2:12; Col. 4:3; Acts 14:27).

"Thou hast a little strength" - This does not mean they were marked by feebleness, but that they were few in number. The Lord's followers were not usually in the majority:

1. Abraham defeated the armies of four kings with 318 men (Gen. 14:14-16).
2. Gideon and his army of 300 put to rout the huge army of the Midianites (Judg. 7:19-23).
3. Elijah was more than a match for the 450 prophets of Baal (I Kings 18:21-40).

These people were also true to the Word of God. They raised no questions about the authority of His Word.

When the Christians were brought before heathen magistrates in times of persecution, they were required to renounce the name of Christ, and to disown Him in a public manner. Then people had stood the test firmly.

The name of Jesus provokes hatred of those who do not love Him (Matt. 10:22; Acts 9:16).

3:9-10 The Defense and the Deliverance

The true church of Christ has very little standing in the eyes of the world. Often she is an object of scorn. Here there were professing Jews who were blaspheming the name of Jesus and persecuting the church. But a change is coming. The opponents of Christ will be compelled to worship at the feet of the church. These people brazenly claimed to be Christians, but their actual character is revealed in no uncertain terms. They are of "the synagogue of Satan." This makes four of the churches that are nests of satanic force (2:9, 13, 24; 3:9).

Because they kept the word of Christ's patience, here is a promise that they would be "kept from the hour of temptation." (Words of my patience is literally "my command to endure.") These people were called upon to endure in the midst of persecution. This passage provides support for the fact that Christ will come for His Church before the time of trial and tribulation described in Rev. 6-19 (I Thes. 5:9).

3:11-13 Declaration and Delight

This is the third time we find it clearly stated that Christ is coming again. Note also how frequently in the Bible His Second Coming is associated with rewards He will give His faithful servants (Rev. 22:12; Matt. 16:27; I Cor. 3:13).

The crown is not our salvation. Here is an admonition to wisely order his life, for he will gain or lose rewards according to his conduct (II Cor. 5:10; II John 8; I Cor. 9:24).

The overcomer (true believer) is promised to be made a "pillar in the temple of God." In Solomon's temple there were two pillars. The right pillar was called Jachin, which means "He will establish." The left pillar was called Boaz, which means "He is my strength" (I Kings 7:15-22). The overcomer will be made a pillar of strength in God's temple. They "shall go no more out," but shall continually dwell in God's presence.

The writing of the name of God is indicative of the fact that the believer is identified with Christ by the seal of the name of God, which entitles him to have entrance into the city of God. In Rev. 21:9-22:6, a new Jerusalem is promised. Here the overcomer (believer) will be established, made permanent, made steadfast in the dwelling house of God forever (Rev. 22:4). This is an eternal seal that they belong to God. The "name of the city" also indicated where the "eternal dwelling house" will be.

We will be identified with the Savior who bought us. He will be identified with His new name, not Jesus. I believe Rev. 19:16 gives His "new name."

VII. Laodicea - The Haughty Church

A.D. 1900 - Rapture

The city of Laodicea was founded by Antiochus II in the middle of the third century B.C. Laodicea was situated about forty miles southeast of Philadelphia on the road to Colossae and Hierapolis, all within a radius of ten miles. Laodicea was by far the largest and wealthiest of the cities. The letter in the Revelation is full of allusions to its riches. The many millions combined to build theaters, huge stadiums, lavish public baths and fabulous shopping centers. Laodicea became legendary for the gold she possessed.

It was a great center of clothing manufacturing. It was world-renowned for the fine quality of its woven garments, produced from a breed of sheep (today extinct) with long, soft, glossy, black wool. Laodicea was also the center of a fine medical school. So famous were its doctors that the names of some of them appear on the coins of Laodicea. The school was famous for ointment for the eyes.

The Laodicean church age began around 1900 and is increasing in intensity at a breath-taking pace. Laodicea could be called the Apostate Ecumenical Church that is gathering momentum at this moment. It is the age of lukewarm Christianity. Christ is seen outside the church, standing at the door and knocking (3:20). His virgin birth, vicarious atonement, and bodily resurrection have been denied by men who claim to be spiritual leaders in Christendom. The meaning of Laodicea is "people's rights." We live in the day when people arise to "claim their rights" to do the judging.

3:14 The Solemn Amen

This reference is to "the church of the Laodiceans." Note with interest that the references to the other churches were "the church in Smyrna: (2:8, 2:12, 2:18, 3:1) etc. This was not the Lord's church, but the Laodecians' church. For this church there is not one word of praise.

"The Amen" is a title for Christ indicating his sovereignty and the certainty of the fulfillment of His promises (II Cor. 1:20). When Christ speaks, it is the final word.

Here is another reference to the "faithful and true witness" (martyr) (1:5, 3:7).

"The beginning of the creation of God" does not mean that Jesus is the first of God's creation, but that Jesus is the original agent in God's creative work (John 1:3; Col. 1:16, 17).

3:15-16 A Serious Apathy

Jesus is saying He knows fully the true condition of the church. His testimony is infallible. He is presenting a true and faithful picture of conditions.

Notice Christ did not say "so then because thou are no longer orthodox and have denied the gospel". Their problem was that they were nauseatingly lukewarm. The word for "hot" is *zestos* which means "hot to a boiling point." They were not ardent Christians. They had no enthusiasm, no emotion, no zeal and no urgency. The word for "cold" is *usuchros* and it means "cold to the point of freezing."

Things which are lukewarm or tepid often have a nauseating effect. Directly across the Lycus River from Laodicea was the Hierapolis. It was famous for its warm mineral springs. Often these mineral springs with their chemical content are nauseating. They would often make the person who drank of them physically sick. This is the way the Laodicean Christians affected Christ.

Here is a group of people who would not take a stand one way or the other toward Christ or the truths of His Word. This is the most hateful, disgusting spirit possible to display against God's work. Total indifference is damning more people today than the liquor traffic, the dope traffic and all other sins combined.

The literal Greek says that because of this sin of indifference "I am about to spew thee out of my mouth." History is swiftly moving to this point.

3:17 The Sinful Apostasy

These are the things of which they boasted: They were rich - her treasury was full. She depended on the deceitfulness of riches. They counted nickels and noses. The dollar was the standard of measurement. They were deluded. They knew not their miserable condition. They possessed no spiritual riches. They were spiritually blind. they were spiritually naked.

3:18-19 The Spiritual Appeal

1. Laodicea prided itself on its financial wealth. It was the banking center of Asia Manor. The Risen Christ advises them to buy gold tried and refined in the fire. Fire is a symbol of the Holy Spirit in the Bible (Matt. 3:11; Acts 2:3). Their gold should be life - refined by the Holy Spirit's fire.
2. Laodicea prided itself on its clothing trade. The garments made at Laodicea were famous all over the world. But the Risen Christ says Laodicea is spiritually naked. This meant more to the ancient world than it does to us. To them, to be naked was the worst humiliation and shame of all. Their

spiritual nakedness was a real shame for all to see. Christ urges them to buy raiment from Him. This is the raiment of righteousness that produces life and character that only Christ can give.

3. Laodicea prided itself on its famous eye-salve. It was exported all over the world. But Laodicea was blind to its own poverty and nakedness. Only Christ, who is the light of the world, could enable them to see - to see their sin and Christ in His Holiness.

Then Jesus makes a reference to these who were believers and belong to Christ, but are out of fellowship with Him. Because of their lukewarm state they are the object of rebuke and chastening of God's judgment. God is saying, "It is the people who are dear to me upon whom I inflict the most severe discipline." If we are not being chastened by the Lord, it could be that we need to look into our relationship to Him.

"REBUKE" (*elegchein*) is a "correction that compels a man to see the error of his ways and admit he is wrong." Rebuke is not so much punishment as illumination.

"CHASTEN" (*paideuo*) means "to train a child." The true believer has an alternative. If he will judge himself and put away his sin, God will not be required in that case to bring chastening upon him. If he will not judge himself, it is clear that God will deal with him.

"BE ZEALOUS" is "to continue to be on fire with zeal and power of the Holy Spirit."

"REPENT" (aorist tense) - make a once-for-all break which lukewarmness and false pride.

3:20 The Savior's Attitude

Here is a vivid picture of Jesus Christ knocking at the door of the Laodicean Church, desiring to enter. If one person in the church will open the door, then Christ will enter and have fellowship with him. There are four basic ways the Lord knocks at the door:

1. Through the Word.
2. Through persons.

3. Through the Holy Spirit.
4. Through providence.

"SUP" is *deipnein.* The Greeks had three meals a day:

1. *Akratisma* (Breakfast) - A piece of dry bread dipped in the fruit of the vine.
2. *Ariston* (Lunch) - A picnic snack eaten by the road or on the job.
3. *Deipnon* - The evening meal where people sat long and talked over the meal. They lingered at unhurried fellowship. This was Christ's reference. No hurried meal - but a lingering fellowship.

3:20-21 The Saintly Attention

The overcomer is to sit on Christ's throne even as Christ sat on His Father's throne.

Revelation Chapter Four

Revelation 1:19 gives the divine outline of the book. He says "Write the things which thou hast seen, the things which are, and the things which shall be hereafter." Revelation 1 is "the things which thou hast seen." Revelation 2 and 3 are "the things which are." Revelation 4-22 deal with "the things which shall be hereafter."

As we begin chapter 4 and continue through our study, there will be two things that will become obvious and impressive:

1. The coming judgment on sin. God has withheld His wrath in ages past but there is coming a time when He will withhold His wrath no longer. Sin will finally be judged.
2. Also, you will be aware of the "Battle of the Ages" that Satan has had with God and His people. This will especially be seen in Rev. 12. An understanding of this chapter is essential to understand the contents of the Book of Revelation. Satan's desire through the ages has been to destroy the nation Israel in general and the Lord Jesus Christ in particular. During the Tribulation, Satan will again attempt to destroy the nation Israel. If he could succeed at this, he could defeat God, for God would not be able to fulfill His promises to Israel. But Christ is victorious. He preserves the nation and brings judgment on Satan.

With chapter 4, our attention is drawn away from the earthly scenes we have been viewing to a beautiful scene in Heaven. We have seen the trials and tribulations of the church on Earth. Now, we see her in all her triumph in glory. Her earthly warfare is ended. She has been translated to receive her rewards. The Bride is complete at last and is presented to the Bridegroom. She is now enthroned in glory with Him.

Those who reject the fact that God still has something in store for Israel must disregard some Scriptures (Acts 15:14-17; Rom. 11:25).

Following the letters to the seven churches of Asia, there is a sharp break in the continuity of the thought. Entirely new matters are discussed, and a proper interpretation of the new situation is the key to the understanding of all that follows in the great symbolic scenes of judgment which are depicted in the rest of the Revelation.

4:1 The Visitation of the Eternal Call

The expression "after this" (*meta tauta*), with which verse one begins, identifies the revelation as subsequent to that of chapter 2 and 3. As he beheld, he saw a door opened into the very presence of God in Heaven. The reference to "Heaven" here is the word for the "third Heaven" which is the very presence of God. This was something John actually saw, not an imagination or fantasy.

John saw the door of the heavenly tabernacle, which was a pattern of the earthly tabernacle (Heb. 8:5; 9:23, 24). It is not unreasonable to believe that this door is literal as pictured here and in Rev. 11:19; 14:15-18; 16:1, 17.

In the early chapters of the Revelation there are three doors, and they are three of the most important doors in life:

1. The door of opportunity (Rev. 3:8).
2. The door of the human heart (Rev. 3:20).
3. The door of Revelation (Rev. 4:1).

There are three instances in the Book of Revelation where Heaven is opened.

1. Rev. 4:1 - This is to admit the Church into Heaven at the Rapture before the Tribulation.
2. Rev. 11:19 - This is opened in the middle of the Tribulation for Israel, God's ancient covenant people. Israel will go through Tribulation. God opens Heaven here to show Israel the Ark of the Covenant in order to encourage them.
3. Rev. 19:11 - This is at the close of the Tribulation when the Lord Jesus returns with His Saints and sets up His Kingdom on Earth.

The "voice like a trumpet" introduces again a simple symbol which frequently occurs from here on in Revelation. This is a symbol of the trumpet - voice of God - suggesting strength and clarity (I Thes. 4:16-17: Rev. 1:10; I Cor. 15:51-52).

The same voice that spoke to John in Rev. 1:10 speaks here and says "come up hither." It is not likely that John was caught away in body. But, because he was "in the Spirit," this indicates that John's spirit for the moment left his body, and his spirit was caught away into Heaven to behold the glorified Lord. John's body was not yet glorified, and no man can behold the beauty and majesty of our glorified Lord in an unredeemed and mortal body.

"Things which must be hereafter." Heaven is the vantage point of all true and accurate prophecy. Man may make predictions of events which are to take place on the Earth, but if those predictions are not from God's point of view they are not to be trusted. The things that are to transpire on Earth have their hidden source in the secret chambers of Heaven. From John's viewpoint as a prisoner on Patmos the picture is dark for the Church and bright for the world which hates her and her Lord. But when John is able to see things from God's point of view, the picture is changed radically. He sees the true church caught up to Heaven, God is on His eternal throne, and manifestations of divine wrath are in store for the Earth dwellers who have rejected His Son. The word "hereafter" makes it clear that what follows is to take place on Earth after the Church Age has run its course.

4:2-3 The Vision of the Enthroned Christ

"Immediately I was in the spirit." The word "immediately" is an adverb of time and means "at once." Not only was John at once in the spirit but was at once in Heaven. This corresponds exactly with the teaching concerning the Rapture which takes place at once (I Cor. 15:52). Even though John was caught up in spirit, the bodies of all saints will be caught up at the Rapture (I Thes. 4:16). This must be the bodies with the spirit, because those who have died already, their spirits have gone to be with the Lord (II Cor. 5:8). Another proof that we will have resurrected (or changed) bodies is: Jesus had a real resurrected body (Luke 24:39). At our resurrection (or change), we will be like Him (I John 3:2).

"A throne was set in Heaven, and one sat on the throne." The book of Revelation uses the word "throne" 45 times. In chapters 4 and 5, which introduce us to the throne room, this word is used 17 times. The throne represents the universal sovereignty and rule of God (Psa. 47:8; 103:19). The word "set" indicates that this throne is permanent.

"And He that sat was to look upon like a Jasper and a Sardine stone." The Jasper stone in Scripture was a clear brilliant transparent stone. The Sardine, on the other hand, was blood-red precious stone much like a ruby. These two stones are used by John to describe the one whom he saw sitting on the throne after he was caught up into Heaven. To understand the meaning of this, we must let Old Testament Scripture give us the meaning.

In Exodus 28, we have Moses giving the children of Israel the pattern of the Tabernacle and the order of the Sanctuary. He also gives minute order concerning the garments of the High Priest. In Ex. 28:15-21 there is given instruction concerning a breastplate of the High Priest with twelve precious stones corresponding to the twelve names of the tribes of the children of Israel, beginning with the oldest, Reuben, and ending with the youngest son, Benjamin. Now see Ex. 28:29.

Here is the picture. The High Priest in the Old Testament Tabernacle carried on his role with the breastplate of judgment immediately over his heart. In it were twelve precious stones arranged in four rows. The first stone was Sardine and had the name of the first-born Reuben on it. The last stone in the last row was a Jasper with the name of Benjamin engraved on it. Between there were the stones of all the other tribes - not one was missing. Everywhere the priest went in the Holy Place, he bore these stones upon his heart as he interceded for Israel and averted judgment by the constant application of the blood from the altar of burnt offering.

We know from the book of Hebrews that Aaron in his priestly office was a type of the Lord Jesus Christ in His priestly intercession for us after His ascension into Heaven.

The one John saw sitting upon the throne in Revelation 4 is described as a Jasper and a Sardine stone. There is a very definite reason for the reversing of the first and last stone. The Sardine stone speaks of Sacrifice and Blood. It pointed to the cross of the "first coming of Jesus Christ" as our Savior. The word "REUBEN" means "behold the Son" (John 1:29). The Jasper, the last stone in the Old Testament Breastplate, was for Benjamin. It was the clear stone of Victory. The name Benjamin means "the Son of my Power." The first and last stones then pointed forward to the first and second coming of the great priest, the Lord Jesus Christ.

The reason for the reversing of the order in the Revelation is simple - the Old Testament saints looked forward to the Cross and therefore saw the Sardine, and red blood stone first and then beyond that the Jasper, the stone of His Second Coming power and rule. But John in Revelation 4 is on this side of the Cross and the Rapture, and therefore in looking back sees first of all the Jasper stone and then beyond that the red stone of the Cross of Sacrifice.

"There was a rainbow round about the throne." The word "RAINBOW" in the Greek is *iris*. It can mean "halo." Here it is Emerald (green). After the judgment of the flood the rainbow appeared as a reminder of God's covenant not to destroy the Earth again with flood (Gen. 9:13-15). It appears here before the judgment of the Great Tribulation as a reminder that a flood will not be used in judgment. Green is the color symbolizing Earth. The rainbow in Rev. 4:3 complete encircles the throne. This emphasizes the completeness of God's mercy, as to the purpose of the rainbow.

4:4-5 THE VISION OF THE ENTHRONED CHURCH

The Elders represent the glorified church translated into Heaven. Twelve is the number for heavenly fullness and administration. The number "twenty-four" would suggest priesthood. All the redeemed are resurrected and received up into mansions of glory. For them it is coronation time.

The word "seats" is also translated "thrones." But, who are the Elders sitting thereupon (Rev. 5:9)? In I Chron. 24 there was an appointment of 24 elders. That was the division of the Levitical priesthood in 24 orders, so each one could minister for "two weeks at a time in the temple that was built." The priesthood numbered thousands and all these priests could not go into the temple at one time; so the priesthood were represented every two weeks by an order of 24 priests (elders). When the 24 were in the temple and were ministering, they were a representative body. What John saw was a representative body, standing for the entire company of men and women who had been washed in the blood of

Jesus Christ. Here is another proof that the church will not go through the Tribulation, for we find these elders in Heaven before the beginning of judgments (Rev. 21:12-14).

The Greek word for "Elder" (*presbuteros*) is used 66 times in the New Testament and is always applied to man - never angels.

The "clothes of white raiment" speak of perfect righteousness (I John 3:2; Phil. 3:20-21; Rev. 7:14).

Why did they have crowns? Because John was projecting into the future and it was as though the judgment seat of Christ had already taken place, and the rewards for service had been given. Of the two Greek words for crown (*diadema* - sovereign's crown; *stephanos* - victor's crown won in games) the one used here is *stephanos* - a crown (rewards) for the victor.

The lightening, thundering and voices which proceed from the throne are prophetic of the righteous judgment of God upon a sinful world. When God was about to visit Egypt's sins upon her, we find an interesting development (Ex. 9:23, 28). When He wished to show Israel the terribleness of His anger with sin, the development is also interesting (Ex. 19:16; I Sam. 7:10; I Sam. 12:17, 18).

The seven lamps of fire represent the fullness and completeness of the Holy Spirit. Here the Holy Spirit takes on His judicial character, fire being a symbol of divine judgment at the Second Coming of Christ to the Earth with His saints (II Thes. 1:7-8). Each member of the Holy Trinity is viewed in connection with the righteous character of the throne. Each is prepared to execute judgment.

4:6

The original Greek here is making a comparison. The statement is not that there was a "sea of glass," but that it looked like a sea of glass. There seems to be an analogy here - or a comparison to - the sea of brass in the Tabernacle in the Wilderness or the molten sea in the Temple. Both were lavers designed for the cleansing of the priests, and contained water used for various ceremonial rites (Ex. 30:18-21; I Kings 7:23-37). Both were used for the purification of the priests and were symbolic of the Word of God. Here the sea is of glass, not of water, for the cleansing is not needed after the church is at home with the Lord. This sea of glass symbolizes the fixed state of holiness and purity of the raptured church (see Rev. 21:11; 22:1).

John occupies himself with the four living creatures around the throne. Their being "full of eyes" before and behind suggests alertness and awareness. They resemble the Cherubim of Ezek. 1:5-10 and the Seraphim of Isa. 6:2-3. The translation of the word "beast" should be "living ones." The word here is *zoon*. If it were "beasts" the word would be *therion* as used in Rev. 13.

4:7

The four "living ones" are representatives of the attributes and qualities of the Lord. Just as the Holy Spirit is represented by seven lamps, the attributes of God are represented by the four "living ones."

The fact that the creatures are full of eyes is taken as significant of the omniscience and omnipresence of God who sees all and knows all. The lion represents majesty and omnipotence. The calf signifies patience and continuous laborer. The "face as a man" represents intelligence and rational power. The eagle represents a symbol of sovereignty and supremacy.

4:8

The first time living creatures are mentioned in the Bible is Gen. 3:24. In the camping and marching order of Israel in the Wilderness, there was a fixed relation of the Twelve Tribes to the Tabernacle.

CAMP OF DANIEL
3 Tribes
Standard bearing figure of an Eagle

CAMP OF EPHRAM		CAMP OF JUDAH
3 Tribes Standard bearing figure of an ox	**The Tabernacle**	3 Tribes Standard bearing figure of a lion

CAMP OF REUBEN
3 Tribes
Standard bearing figure of a man

These creatures do not represent the church, but are officials attached to the Throne of God (Rev. 6:1-8; Rev. 15:7). They give glory and honor and thanks to Him that sits upon the throne. I believe they represent Jesus Christ.

1. The first was "like a lion." A lion is "King of the beasts" and represents majesty and omnipotence. The first is representative of Christ the King as the Gospel of Matthew presents Him.
2. The second was "like a calf." The same word is translated "bullock" or "ox" elsewhere. This was an animal frequently used for sacrifice. The calf-like creature represents Christ as our sacrifice. Mark's Gospel presents Christ as the Servant who was to be sacrificed for us.
3. The third had "a face as a man." This figure represents Christ as a man. Luke presents Christ as a Perfect Man.
4. The fourth was "like a flying eagle." This represents Christ as sovereignty and supremacy - or Christ in all His Deity. John's Gospel presents Christ as the Divine Son of God.

These living creatures do not rest day or night as they protect the throne of God in its holiness and majesty.

Their words of praise are most descriptive and magnificent. The idea of "holiness" is basic to the Bible. This word stands in opposition to that which is common or profane. It means separation from evil. Notes these three things:

1. The Lord Jesus is called Holy (Luke 1:35; 4:34: John 6:69; II Cor. 5:21; I Pet. 2:22; I John 3:5).
2. God's Spirit is called the "Holy Spirit" (Psa. 51:11; Isa. 63:10; Luke 1:35; John 14:26; Acts 1:8).
3. God's Word is Holy (II Tim 3:15; Psa. 19:8, 9; Rom. 1:2; II Pet. 1:21).

4:9-11 The Vision of the Endless Chorus

4:9

What a scene of holy worship we have here. The Living Creatures and The Glorified Body of Christ uniting in the grand anthem of praise.

4:10

As the sound of the "Holies" coming from the four living creatures, the twenty-four Elders rise from their thrones and fall before the triune God to join the ascription of Praise. All of Heaven now gives honor to Him. All of creation bows in adoration to Him. Now true worship exists. John here uses a picture which the ancient world would know well. He says that the Elders cast their crowns before the throne of God. In the ancient world that was a sign of complete submission. When one king surrendered to another king, he cast his crown at the victor's feet.

The God of all creation is now praised and not blasphemed. In Heaven we will then know the joy of having been created. Friend, there are no songs of evolution in Heaven - only songs of creation. Jesus Christ is the agent of all creation (John 1:3; Col. 1:16).

Revelation Chapter Five

This chapter, like the first, forms an introduction to another division of Revelation. It introduces the supernatural judgment about to be poured out upon the Earth. We are not to gaze upon the throne but upon the One who occupies the throne. He is the center of all interest and adoration. The throne is the seat of authority. The Seven Sealed Scroll is the record of that authority. His rights, prerogatives and program are found in the book. But the one who occupies the throne is the Person of Authority. His judgments are final - His Word infallible.

5:1 The Scroll of Judgment

The secret of God's judgments are about to be revealed. The Greek word here for "book" is "scroll" - a roll of parchment sealed with seven seals. The word is "Biblion" from which we get our word "BIBLE". The importance of this document is revealed by the fact that it is "written on both sides." It is also made impressive by seven seals, apparently fixed on the edges of the scroll in such a way that the seals must be successively broken if the scroll is to be unrolled and read.

We are told that the book is "sealed with seven seals." "Seven" refers to perfection and completion. God is emphasizing that this is final.

5:2-4 The Search for a Justice

The reference here introduces a subject that we want to discuss in our Revelation studies - that of Angelology.

ANGELOLOGY

I. Angels as Personalities

- A. Angels are created, not begotten (Heb. 1:5-14; Col. 1:16).
    1. They do not procreate and marry (Matt. 22:30).
    2. They do not experience death (Luke 20:36).
    3. They are a spirit (Heb. 1:14).

4. They can appear as human form when necessary (Gen. 18:1-8; Heb. 13:2).

B. Angels may be seen by beasts (Num. 22:22-31).

C. Angels have superhuman powers (Judg. 13:19, 20; II Pet. 2:11; Psa. 103:20).

D. Angels are free moral agents.

1. They are "holy" (Luke 9:26).

2. Yet, they are free moral agents (Ezek. 28:14-16; II Pet. 2:24; Jude 6).

E. Angels are limited in knowledge (I Pet. 1:12; Matt. 24:36).

F. Angels accompany the spirit of the deceased believer into Heaven (Luke 16:22).

G. Angels have names (Heb. 1:4; Dan. 10:13).

H. Angels are inferior to Jesus in worship (Heb. 1:6; Col. 2:18, 19).

II. Angels Witnessed Creation (Job 38:1-7) (See Job 1:6 & 2:1).

III. Angels are Used by God to Make Things Happen.

A. Hagar (Gen. 16:1-11; Gen. 21:14-20).

B. Abraham (Gen. 22:11-12).

C. An Angel acts as cupid (Gen. 24:7)!

D. Lot (Gen. 19:1).

E. Jacob (Gen. 28:11-16; Gen. 48:15, 16).

F. Children of Israel (Ex. 23:20, 23).

G. Elizah (I Kings 19:1-8).

H. Daniel (Dan. 6:16-23).

I. Zechariah (Zech. 1:8, 9).

J. Peter (Acts 12:1-11).

IV. Angels are Heaven's "Special Delivery Service."

A. Judg. 13:3-5

B. Dan. 9:20-23

C. Luke 1:11-17

D. Luke 1:28-33

E. Matt. 1:18-21

F. Matt. 2:13, 19, 20

V. Angels in Evangelism.

A. The Gospel was introduced by angels (Luke 2:10-11; Matt. 1:21).

B. The Resurrection was confirmed by angels (Matt. 28:6-7).
C. The Angels can direct in witnessing (Acts. 8:25, 26; Acts 10:1-6).
D. An angel saves an evangelist (Acts 27:23-25).

VI. Angels as Energizers.

A. Ministering to Jesus (Luke 4:14, 15; Luke 22:43, 44).
B. Ministering in healing (John 5:4).
C. Ministering to Daniel (Dan. 10:1-3, 8, 16, 18).

VII. Angels as Protectors (Psa. 34:7; Psa. 91:11, 12).

A. Daniel in the lion's den.
B. Hebrew children from fiery furnace.
C. Isaac from his Father's knife.
D. Promise of angelic protection for children (Matt. 18:10).

5:2-4 The Search for a Justice

The Angel of the Lord proclaims which a "loud voice" concerning the worthiness of one to open the book. Here this angel is a herald or crier. Here the Lord is impressing the mind with a sense of the importance of the disclosures about to be made. That one of the highest angels should make such a proclamation would sufficiently show his importance.

Here John records in verse 3 that no one in Heaven, in Earth, or under the Earth was WORTHY (*edynoto* - to have power or authority) to open the book. Notice who needs to open the book - not someone who is strong, but someone who is "WORTHY." The only worthy one is the Lord Jesus Christ.

The failure to find anyone who qualified to open the book shows the moral inability of man. The philosophy of the world is that we can get along with God. The incident of the seven-sealed book shows us that there are many things that only God can do.

John enters the picture here because he had come from Earth. John realized that he was not worthy to open the book. As an Israelite, the Apostle John knew the significance of the seven-sealed book. He knew it spelled out the complete, final redemption of man, of Israel and of Earth. As he considered that no man in Heaven or Earth was worthy to open the book, he wept. The tense of the verb shows that John "continuously wept."

5:5-7 The Sovereign Judge

These words of the elder and the appearance of the "Lamb as it was slain," instantly relieved John's agonizing suspense, as well as that of all beings of Heaven. When the Lamb had taken the book, worship to Him began with the living creatures and elders and reached throughout all creation. Now the book will be opened!

Christ is here described as the "Lion of the tribe of Judah." Dying Jacob utters the first prophecy which thus describes Him (Gen. 49:8-10; Heb. 7:14).

He was also described as "the Root of David" (Isa. 11:1,10; Rev. 22:16; II Sam. 7:12-16).

Notice the words "hath prevailed" in verse 5. The thought here is that He has acquired this power as a conflict or struggle. The conflict in which He was the victor was the conflict of Calvary.

Here in verse 6 is the supreme moment of this vision - the emergence of the Lamb in the scene of Heaven. John says the Lamb was the center of the whole scene - the focus of every eye (I Pet. 1:18-19; John 1:29, 36; Isa. 53:7; Jer. 11:19).

It was this Lamb, then, who came and took the scroll from the right hand of the One on the throne. When He had done so, the judgments were about to begin. As we shall see, this scene will strike terror into the hearts of men, as they shall attempt to hide from the One on the throne and "from the wrath of the Lamb" (Rev. 6:16).

Here again we have the number 7 denoting fullness, completion and perfection. The horn stands for authority and imperial power of complete dominion. Christ possesses it, and now He steps forth to exercise it, perfectly equipped to put down any opposition to His Kingdom (Matt. 28:18).

In the Old Testament the horn stands for three things:

1. Sheer power (Deut. 33:17; I Kings 22:11; Zech. 1:18-19).
2. Honor (I Sam. 2:1; Psa. 89:17; Psa. 148:14).
3. Authority (Literature between the testament).

The eyes stand for perception. Seven eyes are "perfect perception."

The "seven Spirits of God" represents the fullness of administration of the Holy Spirit in God's government (Zech. 4:10). Clearly, this also stands for the all-seeing omniscience of God.

In verse 7 we come to one of the most climatic passages of all history. This is the act whereby the Lord Jesus Christ takes the book from the One on the throne. Christ is no longer seen as Intercessor of the Church, for the Church at this time is in His presence. He is now beginning to act as Judge.

There are three laws of Redemption in the Old Testament that we need to examine at this point.

1. The Law of Redemption concerning a wife (Deut. 25:5-10). Jesus, with His own blood, redeemed the Bride (the true Church) and fulfilled the position as Brother (Rev. 1:5).
2. The Law of Redemption concerning a slave (Lev. 25:35-55). When he served six years as a slave, he was automatically freed on the seventh. (It is interesting to note that during Creation, God worked six days and on the seventh He rested (See II Pet. 3:8). We have had about six thousand years of human history. It must be about time, on God's clock, for peace and rest to begin).
3. The Law of Redemption concerning the land (Lev. 25:23-25). This redemption will be accomplished when Jesus comes with His saints (Dan. 7:13-14).

5:8-10 The Song of Joy

5:8

The four living creatures and the twenty-four elders, representing the saved people, fell down in adoration before the Lord. This is the moment for which all creation has been waiting and longing. The nation of Israel has been waiting for the fulfillment of the 70th week of Daniel, so the Kingdom of God can be established on Earth. The saints of the Church

Age have prayed and suffered and waited for almost 2,000 years for God to vindicate them.

The first action of this supreme moment is the transference of the reins of government to the slain Lamb. The creatures and the elders have harps which are instruments of divine worship, and they possess and pour out golden vials full of odors which are declared to be the prayers of the saints. The Son of God now gets His rightful worship.

The "golden vials" are marked by their value and attests to the high and holy service for which they are used. The incense in the vials are "the prayers of the saints." Prayer on Earth is incense in Heaven. God in His own inimitable way and rich grace values our cries and intercessions, and they ascend to Him as incense (Psa. 141:2).

5:9

They sang a new song. There is no song recorded in the book of Genesis. The patriarchs were men of deep thought and of serious mind. The first song on Earth of which we have any account is narrated in Exodus 15. The deliverance which had been wrought for Israel formed the material for the song (Ex. 15:1).

The song in our text is termed "new" because of its theme - redemption actually accomplished. Note that there is no song in Chapter 4. There we all bow and worship Him.

The Greek language has two words for "new."

1. *Neos*- New in point of time, but not necessarily new in point of quality.
2. *Kainos* - New in that the like of which has never existed before.

Here the word for "new" is *Kainos*.

The praise that is rendered to the Lamb by the four living creatures and by the elders is rendered to Him because He died. In this song there is summed up the results for us of the death of Jesus Christ.

1. The death of Christ was a sacrificial death!
2. The death of Christ was an emancipating death! (Mark 11:45; I Tim. 2:6; I Pet. 1:19)

3. The death of Christ was an availing death.
   a. He made us kings (Rev. 1:6).
   b. He made us priests (I Pet. 2:5, 9).
   c. He gave us victory (I Cor. 15:57).

5:10

To the saints who are the kings and priests we have the simple affirmation that they will reign on Earth. This is a reference to the earthly millennial reign of Christ in which the church will participate.

5:11-12 The Sacrifice of Jesus

5:11

In an area beyond that which was occupied by the throne, the angels, living creatures and elders are giving their praise to Him and rejoicing in His praise and glory. Here is a countless number of creatures praising the Lord (Dan. 7:10).

5:12

As the host of worshippers declare the Lamb to be worthy, they ascribe to Him a sevenfold combination of attributes:

1. Strength (Rev. 20:3, 10)
2. Riches (II Cor. 8:9)
3. Wisdom (Col. 2:3)
4. Power (I Cor. 1:24; Matt. 28:18)
5. Honor (John 17:5; Phil. 2:11)
6. Glory (John 17:5; 1:14)
7. Blessing (Psa. 103:1-2)

5:13-14 The Supreme Jubilation

5:13

Now the praise goes as far as it possibly can, for it reaches throughout the whole of the universe and the whole creation (Psa. 148:7-13).

5:14

So in the closing scene of Revelation 5, the four living creatures say "Amen," and the four and twenty elders fall down and worship Him. Universal homage is paid to the One upon whom is focused all of God's purpose for time and eternity.

Revelation Chapter Six

The attention of the reader is now called away from the glories of Heaven to the scenes on Earth. The awful day has dawned. Day of wrath and judgment. This period of time we have under consideration we call the Tribulation or Daniel's 70th Week.

We are about to enter an examination of the strictly prophetic part of the book, and we do so with this fact before us, that through different judgments - Seals, Trumpets, Vials - have their place in the internal between our gathering to the Lord Himself, (the Rapture) and His and our manifestation to the world at the close of Daniel's last prophetic week (The Second Coming).

The Church is expressly promised exemption from the Tribulation (Rev. 3:10; I Thes. 1:10).

Chapter 6 continues the vision, again with no break in the thought; and we follow the events, through the eyes of John, as, one after another, the lion of the tribe of Judah breaks the seven seals and opens the scroll.

This period is presented under the heading of the Seven Seals, the Seven Trumpets, the Seven Personages, the Seven Vials, and the Seven Dooms. These events do not occur in successive manner. They are not in sequence, but they occur simultaneously and parallel each other and often intermingle.

It will be well for us to remember here the Law of Recurrence. This law is that principle of rhetoric by which the Holy Spirit first states a fact in outline, then refers to it again and again to add details.

Terrible indeed those days and terrifying the events befalling the Earth. Although the twice-born have been removed, the teaming multitudes upon the Earth will continue on in the same way. Business as usual. Apostate Church is still on the Earth. Evil will increase unhindered by the restraining power of the Holy Spirit.

The Tribulation is triggered from Heaven. Jesus Christ directs the entire operation. There are certain factors that are brought in focus which increase the intensity and ferocity of the Tribulation:

1. The Holy Spirit restrains evil no longer. He is taken from Earth (II Thes. 2:7).
2. The true Church (Body of Christ), as light and salt is removed from the Earth in Rapture (I Thes. 4:13-18).
3. The devil knows that he has but a short time remaining.
4. Evil men are new free to carry out their nefarious plans (Matt. 24:37-39).
5. There is direct judgment from God (Rev. 6:17).

Before we take up this study in some detail, let us note first that chapter 6 tells of the opening of six of the seals. Then a parenthesis follows in chapter 7; and the breaking of the seventh seals, as recorded in 8:1, 2 introduces the seven trumpet judgments. In like manner, as we shall see later, six of the trumpet judgments are described in chapters 8 and 9; while another parenthesis follows in 10:1 - 11:14. The seventh trumpet judgment is pictured in 11:15-18. And in the same manner, the six bowls of the wrath of God are described in 15:1-16. Then follows a brief parenthesis in 16:13-16, before the seventh angel pours out his vial into the air.

6:1-2 The Conquest (The First Seal - A White Horse)

6:1

We are now entering the first half of Daniel's 70th Week, the seven year period of Tribulation. All the acts described under the seven seals are acts of judgment. The scene is a judgment scene. The throne is a judgment throne. It will be well for us to note the origin of this vision (Zech. 6:1-8).

As each of the seven seals is broken and opened a new terror falls upon the Earth. The first terror is depicted under the form of a white horse and its rider. In this preliminary announcement of coming judgment there is fullness and a precision of statement not found in the opening of the remaining six Seals, or even the first Trumpet and the first Vial. Here the cardinal One is used, and not the ordinal FIRST, as in all others. This is very unusual and is ascribed to this one scene alone.

John heard "as it were the noise of thunder." The thundering voice speaks of coming judgment. Thunder portends a coming storm (Ex. 9:23).

John is summoned to come and look upon the scene before him. In this verse we see that the one giving the command is "one of the four beasts" (living creatures).

6:2

The "white horse rider" is the most controversial figure in Scripture. There are those who feel that this rider is the Lord Jesus who goes forth on a career of conquest. This conclusion is drawn, because this picture is connected with the picture in Rev. 19:11, 12. It is to be noted that the crown is the *stephanos* , which is the victor's crown. In Rev. 19, the crown is the *diadema*, which is the royal crown. The passage which we are studying is a passage which is telling of woe upon woe and disaster upon disaster, and any picture of the Risen and Victorious Lord is out of place. The picture tells of the coming of the terrors of the wrath of God on the world.

I believe this rider is the Antichrist. He is the counterfeit superman, the wicked one to appear after the Church is translated (II Thes. 2:8). This rider is Satan's man. His weapon is a bow; Christ's weapon is a sword. He comes imitating Christ and offering peace, but he is as false as is the peace he offers. His golden age is short lived.

The part of the world over which the Antichrist, who is the "little horn" of Daniel 7, the man of Sin, the Beast of Rev. 13, the ruler of the restored Roman Empire, and the final world dictator, will be the old Roman Empire. He will consolidate Europe, reviving the Roman Empire, and will go forth to conquer. (The World Trade Federation has almost already done this.)

This "man of sin" will have three great antagonists: the king of the north, the king of the south, and the confederacy of the eastern nations. Let me say that when north, south, east or west is referred to in the Bible; they are always in relation to Palestine.

During this period of time there will be four confederacies: (1) The Roman Empire, under the Antichrist, (2) those European nations that were not in the old Roman Empire, under the last ruler of Russia, the king of the north, (3) Egypt, taking in the surrounding territory in North Africa, under the leadership of the king of the south; and (4) the nations under the leadership of the "kings of the east" (Oriental).

Hand-to-hand conflict demands the use of the sword, a little distance off; the spear; more distant warfare is expressed by the bow. This latter weapon would not do much execution; hence its employment as a symbol of war afar off, and that not of a very deadly character. Since no arrows are mentioned, this indicated a cold war rather than any actual fighting.

This rider of the white horse goes forth in a mighty conquest and he is victorious - the white horse is a symbol of victory. He is victorious without bloodshed or slaughter. This rider has a bow no arrows. In the Bible, when was fought with a bow and arrow, the arrow was specifically mentioned (Num. 24:8; Psa. 45; Zech. 9:14).

A crown was given unto him. The word mentioned here is the word for "victor's crown." The crown here was "given" (not earned) as significant that he would be victorious - not that he had been. It is not said by whom that was given, just the fact that it was given.

He went forth conquering, and to conquer. This is victory after victory - conquest without defeat.

6:3-4 The Conflict (The Second Seal - The Red Horse)

The peace which the rider on the white horse brought to the Earth was counterfeit and temporary. The Antichrist presents himself as a ruler who brings peace to the world - but he cannot guarantee it, for God says there is no peace to the wicked (Isa. 57:21).

6:3

The Apostle John continues to describe the opening of the seals. Here the Lamb is still with the book in His hand and breaking the seal as He had done with the first one.

The white horse denotes a series of peaceful victories. The red horse initiates a period of slaughter and bloodshed. One of the most terrible wars in man's history will now become a reality.

6:4

The wickedness of men has been so great that God allows a leader among them to carry out His judgment upon them. The rider is unnamed. Power was given to him to bring sorrow and distress upon man because of his sin. The real intent of the Antichrist is revealed with the opening of the second seal. He is to actually take peace from the Earth, not give it!

This is the first battle of the greatest global conflict the world has ever known. This conflict will culminate in the last great battle of Armageddon which will be brought to an end by Christ Himself.

According to our Lord's teaching, the end of this age will be marked by "wars and rumors of wars" (Matt. 24:6).

When the red horse rider appears, men will have grown careless. They will be talking "peace and safety," then destruction will come upon them suddenly (I Thes. 5:3). The rider of the red horse will take peace from the Earth.

Red is the color associated with terror, bloodshed and death. In Revelation we have the red horse (6:3-4), the red dragon (12:3), and the red beast (17:3). Keep in mind that the Holy Spirit is taken from the Earth, so the slaughter is infused into men by satanic power. (It is appropriate to note that Communism today has its color as Red - and are called Reds!).

A great sword given to the rider intimidates that the broils and commotion which he brings about will be marked by great bloodshed.

6:5-6 The Cry for Food (The Third Seal - A Black Horse)

6:5

With the opening of the third seal the same rider appears on a black horse. This time he holds no weapon of warfare in his hands, but a pair of balance scales. These balances, like the black horse, suggests scarcity to the extent of famine. Famine always follows war. During the tribulation men will know what it means to go hungry. All the world will feel the impact of starvation.

Black is the color of famine (Lam. 5:10; Jer. 14:1-2). The two main staff of life are to be called out by weight and sold at famine prices. The rider with the balances speaks of "food conservation" — a term fresh in the minds of everyone. World scientists are saying that world famine is inevitable in a few years.

To "eat bread by weight" in the Scriptures is always a sign of great scarcity (Lev. 26:26; Ezek. 4:16).

6:6

One in the midst of the four beasts proclaimed that there would be such a state of things that a measure of wheat would be sold for a denarius. Three measures of barley would be sold for a denarius. A measure was a *choinix* - or equivalent to two pints, and in the ancient world was one man's ration for a day. A denarius was a working man's wage for a day. John is saying a man's whole working wage would have to be spent in buying enough wheat for him for a day (and we think a dollar-a-loaf for bread is bad). If he bought inferior barley, he might have some for his wife and family.

You will notice that he says to "hurt not the oil and wine." Oil and wine were luxuries of the rich. It seems that the judgment for the rich will be delayed a little longer, but it will come (James 5:1). The olive trees and grape vines need no cultivation, hence their ruthless destruction by the invaders is forbidden. The oil and wine could be protected also because of medicinal purposes after the great war (Luke 10:34).

6:7-8 The Companions (The Fourth Seal - A Pale Horse)

The last of the horsemen is mentioned with the opening of the fourth seal. This is the judgment of wholesale death upon the Earth.

The picture is a grim one. The horse is pale in color. The word is *chloros*, which means a livid, ashy-pale condition. The color is one that signifies a person in death.

This is the only one of the four horsemen named. Here the name of the horseman is Death. Hell (Hades) follows along to receive those who have been cut off by death. At the close of the thousand years reign, they both will be cast permanently into the lake of fire (Rev. 20:14). Here death and Hell are inseparable companions. Together they act in judgment and divide the spoil. Death takes the body and Hell takes the spirit (Luke 16:23).

At the Great White Throne of Judgment, death will be destroyed, praise the Lord (I Cor. 15:26; Rev. 21:4)! The Christian can take heart. Because of his being in Christ he need not fear death or Hell (Rev. 1:18).

The authority to kill and destroy was not his, but was given to him (Death). By any standard of comparison, this is an awesome judgment. If one fourth of the world's population is destroyed, it will represent the greatest destruction of human life ever recorded. At today's population that would be about one billion people. It would mean more than the population of Europe and South America today.

We live in a day when this could easily become a reality. We now possess the Atom and Hydrogen bombs, plus bacteria bombs that are capable of wiping out a large segment of the population within hours. Praise the Lord, I don't have to be a part of this (I Thes. 1:10).

Here there are four instruments of judgment. It is interesting to note that they are the same instruments with which Jehovah threatened Jerusalem of old (Ezek. 14:21).

6:9-11 The Christians Martyred (The Fifth Seal)

6:9

In the fifth seal the scene shifts from Earth to Heaven and John sees a vision of those who will be martyred for their faith in Christ. They are described as being under the altar, in keeping with the fact that the blood of the sacrifices of the Old Testament was poured out under the altar (Lev. 4:7). These are people who will be saved after the rapture but who paid for their testimony with their lives. Their murderers will still be alive on the Earth and will be later judged.

The fact that their souls were under the "Sacrifice Altar" is proof that they had been offered as a "Sacrifice," that is that they were Martyrs. But they are not the Martyrs of the Church Age, for they will be resurrected and taken up with the Church. Then Martyrs are those who will be killed after the Rapture takes place. These are martyrs of the first half of the Tribulation who repudiated the Antichrist and refuse his prescribed form of religion.

Jesus, before He left Earth, left no doubt in His followers as to the suffering which some would endure (Matt. 24:9, 10). The day would come when those who killed the Christians would think they were doing a service for God (John 16:2).

The souls are beneath the altar, the place of safety and security. The lifeblood of the martyrs has been poured out as an offering and a sacrifice to God. These martyred people, who have been slain, are pictured as "souls."

This brings up a Bible doctrine not often discussed. This passage reveals that a soul is a bodily shape, which is shaped like the "body of flesh." This "soul," being the seat of the emotion, is a bodily shaped, invisible type of "spirit." In Luke 16, the rich man in Hades had a tongue, eyes, voice - and yet his physical body is in the grave. The "soul" in the Bible must have a bodily shape - invisible to man's eyes - and it leaves the body at death (Gen. 35:18; II Tim 4:6; Phil. 1:23; Matt. 10:28).

The reasons for the death of these martyrs are plainly set forth. They were "slain for the Word of God, and for the testimony which they hold." These believers were either starved (because they refused the mark of the beast) or were murdered outright for their faith.

In the Tribulation there will be a continuing testimony to Christ through the Word. Even though the Holy Spirit has been removed from the Earth (II Thes. 2:1-7), as a permanent restraining force, Scripture nowhere says He will not come back periodically to people (as in the Old Testament) and do His saving work with those who exercise faith in the Word (Rom. 10:17).

These who die under the fifth seal are true martyrs because of the reason for their being slain. The Bible they have in their possession will be the divinely inspired and infallible Word of God. The prevailing spirit of the time will be one of rebellion against the Bible. This will be a major cause of the world's hatred against them.

6:10

They plead that their blood might be avenged. The attitude of the Tribulation martyrs marks the change in dispensation. We in the dispensation of grace must deal with others in grace as God dealt with us. The tribulation saints will be living in the dispensation of judgment, thus they pray according to the ruling principle of that period of time in which they find themselves.

6:11

In answer to their question, the Lord gives them a white robe as an emblem or symbol of purity and innocence; of divine approval of their testimony and lives, and a pledge of their future blessedness.

These souls were comforted, and they were told to rest for a "little season" - about 3 1/2 years - until their fellow servants were killed as they. It is my belief that most - if not all - of those who will be martyred for Christ during the Tribulation will be Jews. This martyrdom will continue until the Tribulation comes to a close.

6:12-17 The Catastrophic Events (The Sixth Seal)

With the opening of the sixth seal we note an alarming increase in the tempo and intensity of the judgments falling on the Earth. Here we have the events that precede the end of the Tribulation. These events are connected with heavenly phenomena in the sun, moon, and stars, and they match the warnings of Jesus in the Gospels (Matt. 24:29; Mark 13:24-26; Luke 21:25).

Now the greatest judgment of God upon this Earth is expressed through nature. God's judgment on man's sin the first time was through nature (the flood). Man's sin brought a curse on Earth (Gen. 3:17-19). Even the ground was cursed because of man's sin (Gen. 4:12). As we have already stated, these eruptions of nature will not begin immediately. They will also be evident during the last days on Earth, and will intensify during the Tribulation (Matt. 24:7; Luke 21:25; Luke 21:26).

We all know that the world has been plagued for many centuries by cosmic disturbances, and interestingly, such things have been on the increase in recent years. Yet the scene described here is of such great intensity and scope that it seems to suggest a major interruption of life as we know it today.

6:12

Here John is using a scene which is very familiar to the Jewish people. They always regarded the end time as a time when the Earth would be shattered, and when there would be cosmic upheaval and destruction. The Great Tribulation both opens and closes with these upheavals in the natural universe.

1. The beginning of the Tribulation (Joel 2:30-31; Acts 2:19-20).
2. At the end of the Tribulation (Joel 3:16; Isa. 13:13; Matt. 24:29).

In our day, earthquakes are on the increase. In 1972 there was one earthquake every three days. The most powerful earthquake is yet to come (Rev. 16:18; Matt. 24:7; Ezek. 38:19).

There are four great earthquakes during the seven years Tribulation which are defined in Revelation.

1. One during the sixth seal which will take place prior to the sealing of the 144,000, the seventh seal, the seven trumpets, and the seven vials (Rev. 6:12).
2. The one that will take place after the loosing of the seventh seal and before the blowing of the first trumpet (Rev. 8:5).
3. The one that will occur under the seventh trumpet in the middle of the Week (Rev. 11:19).
4. The one that will occur at the time of the ascension of the witnesses (Rev. 11:13; 16:17-21; Zech. 14:4-8).

Note the word "as" which is a word of comparison. The sun did not actually become sackcloth of hair but it looked as if it did. The actual meaning is that on Earth there is thick, dense darkness. There are three times in Bible history when the Earth became black and dark (Gen. 1:2; Ex. 10:21-23; Matt. 27:45).

There are five times that the sun or part of it will be darkened during the Tribulation.

1. This one during the sixth seal in the early part of the Tribulation (Rev. 6:12).
2. During the fourth trumpet, one-third of the sun will be darkened (Rev. 8:12).
3. During the fifth trumpet the sun will be darkened by smoke from the pit (Rev. 9:2).
4. During the fifth vial, in the last of the Tribulation, the sun will be darkened again (Rev. 16:10).
5. "Immediately at the close of the Tribulation" it will be darkened (Matt. 24:29; Isa. 13:10; Ezek. 32:7; Joel 2:31).

The moon, perhaps, will be caused to look as blood by smoke and vapor that accompany an earthquake. Also, an atomic or hydrogen explosion will cause a like affect.

6:13

Also during the Tribulation there will be a shower of meteors that will bring devastation to Earth. The stars will fall as untimely figs when she is shaken of a mighty wind.

6:14

The picture here in the Revelation itself is a picture of a scroll stretched out and held open, and then suddenly split down the middle, and each half recoils and rolls up (Isa. 34:4). This is a reference to the firmament or atmospheric Heaven.

Then there will be the literal movement of every mountain and island. The word "as" is not used here (Jer. 4:24). Ezekiel prophesied that after a group of nations headed by Russia will move into the middle east against the people of Israel and God would shake every mountain and island (Ezek. 38:19-20).

6:15

A universal fear now engulfs the world. These seven groups include the whole fabric of human society. No one is exempt from the judgment of God (Isa. 2:11-12).

6:16

These sinners on Earth will be filled with mortal fear. They will cry for the rocks and mountains to fall on them and hide them from the face of Him that sits upon the throne. What these people dread most is not death, but the revealed presence of God. At this point they no longer deny God or the wrath of God. They realize the day has come when they will meet Him face to face.

6:17

This chapter closes with a question, "Who is able to stand?" This should make the sinner think and consider his way. No one can stand in God's presence unless he stands clothed in the righteousness of Christ.

The Olivet Discourse by the Lord Jesus Christ in Matthew 24 is an answer to the question by His disciples, "What shall be the sign of the end of the age?" The present age does not end with the rapture of the church, but ends with the glorious, victorious return of the Lord with

His saints to close the Tribulation and usher in the next age - the Millennium.

In verse 15 of Matthew 24 is seen the first half of the tribulation period as revealed in Chapter 6 of Revelation.

Matthew 24	Revelation 6
1. False Christ (v. 5)	1. Seal One (v. 1, 2)
2. Wars (v. 6, 7)	2. Seal Two (v. 3, 4)
3. Famine (v. 7)	3. Seal Three (v. 5, 6)
4. Pestilence (v. 7)	4. Seal Four (v. 7, 8)
5. Kingdom Preaching (v. 14)	5. Seal Five (v. 9)
6. Martyrdom (v. 9)	6. Seal Six (v. 9, 10)
7. Earthquake (v. 7)	7. Seal Seven (v. 12)

Revelation Chapter Seven

This chapter is a parenthesis between the sixth and the seventh seals. When the seventh seal is to be opened, it will usher in judgment so terrible and destruction so complete that except those days are shortened, no flesh should be saved. This seventh chapter of Revelation records how God is going to keep and protect His people in the midst of this Tribulation.

This relation between a seal and protection from judgment is paralleled in Ezekiel's prophecy (Ezek. 9:3-6). So, in Revelation judgment was to be withheld until 144,000 persons have been sealed. Who are these people? On the basis of the description one may conclude that it was a group of Jewish people, for they were composed of 12,000 from each of the twelve tribes of Israel. Later in our study we shall see that "the beast," who oppose God and His people, also sealed his followers that they might be known (Rev. 13:16-17; 14:9).

As has already been stated, chapter seven is a parenthesis. The Lamb does not open the seventh seal until chapter eight. Were we to omit chapter seven entirely and begin reading at 8:1, we would have a running narrative and a completed picture of the seal judgments. The parenthesis is put here by the Lord for a reason.

When we go to Revelation seven the 144,000 Jews are sealed. So Revelation seven is telling you something that takes place during the six seals. The chronology then closes with the seventh seal at the beginning of Revelation eight.

How much confusion would be avoided if we will not lose sight of two great facts:

1. This chapter cannot have application to the Church on Earth, nor to the church in glory, for the simple reason that the church is already complete and translated to glory.

2. The vision states clearly that the sealed company is "of all the tribes of the Children of Israel."

The sealed company is of Israel. After the church is removed to glory, when the fullness of the Gentiles is complete (Rom. 11:25-26), the Lord will turn in mercy to Israel and call a remnant which will also be sealed. This remnant is frequently seen on the pages of Old Testament prophecy. This remnant, enlightened by the word of God, will pass through the entire Tribulation period. Many of them will suffer martyrdom, but the greater part will pass through the Tribulation, enduring to the end, and then taken by the Lord when He comes in glory to close the Tribulation period.

In Matt. 3:1, John preached, "The Kingdom of Heaven is at hand." John's message was strictly that a kingdom was to be set up and the King was coming. But the Jews refused to have Jesus reign over them. They said, "Let His blood be upon us and our children." They have had a bloodbath ever since. They rejected the Kingdom's message and her King — and God turned to the Gentiles. Read carefully Romans 11. Unless you understand Rom. 11, it is difficult to understand the message of the Kingdom. The Jews have been set aside (except as Grace has been offered) - but only for a season. But God has not forsaken the Jew. The message of the Kingdom will be preached again right here on Earth - by the 144,000 sealed ones (Matt. 24:12). Today we are preaching the Gospel of Grace. This is the age of Grace, not the Kingdom Age.

During the days of Elijah, God reserved 7,000 who did not bow their knee to Baal (I Kings 19:18). God has always had His faithful witness and He always will. This 144,000 will not be sealed by the Holy Spirit as we are today (Eph. 4:30). These will be sealed with a seal in their foreheads (Matt. 24:31).

In studying this seventh chapter of Revelation you will note that there are two major groups of saints in the Tribulation. The opening portion of the chapter pictures the 144,000 - the godly remnant of Israel on Earth. The latter part of this chapter describes a great multitude of martyred dead in Heaven. Those who died as a testimony to their faith from every kindred, tongue and nation. It is very clear that there will be people saved during the Tribulation. There is no Scripture that indicates otherwise.

7:1-3 The Suspension of Judgment (The Staying of the Angels)

The opening of the sixth seal brings men to the recognition that God is sitting in judgment upon the Earth. This seal is the announcement that the day of immediate judgment is at hand, and the seventh seal is the actual beginning of that day. Between these two seals, dispensing of judgment is arrested long enough to reveal grace, mercy - operating in the midst of judgment. The events of this parenthetical inset reach back to the beginning of the Tribulation period, and forward to the close of it.

7:1

These angels are the good angels, for "another angel" is to speak to them of "our" God. "Four corners of the Earth" means "four directions" (Matt. 24:31; Rev. 20:8). "Holding the winds" refers to a "firm grip" keeping the winds from struggling to get loose. The powers and forces of evil are effectively bridled until the plans of God are ripe and ready for action. The winds here refer to the judgments of God which the trumpet angels hold and will be poured out immediately after the seventh seal. In many places in Scriptures, the wind is used as the symbol for judgment and in the fact that there are four winds that the judgment is worldwide (Jer. 49:36).

In regard to the meaning of the symbol here employed there can be no great difficulty as to the application. The winds are the proper symbols of war and commotion. No winds are to blow up the Earth which is symbolized as governments, no wind is to blow upon the sea which is symbolic of peoples; nor upon any trees which might be the pride of the Earth.

The essential ideas, therefore, in this portion of Scripture are twofold: (1) That at the period of time here referred - after the opening of the sixth seal and before the opening of the seventh - there would be a state of things which would be well represented by rising tempests and storms, which if unrestrained would spread desolation afar; and (2) that this impending ruin was held back as if by angels having control of those winds - those tempests were not suffered to go forth to spread desolation over the world.

7:2

The angel referred to in our test is evidently a distinguished spiritual creature having an exalted mission on hand. This fifth angel directed the four angels in their work over nature, showing that the fifth angel has an official and directive position. This confirms that angels are divided into ranks.

The "seal of the living God" means that which God has appointed, or that which He would use. This seal was entrusted to an angel, who was authorized to use it, and whose use of it would be sanctioned and directed by the living God, as if he had employed it Himself.

"Cried with a loud voice" is *phone megale*. It is our word for megaphone. This voice is so powerful that the world can hear the message. This is a voice of authority.

7:3

The Great Tribulation will be held back until certain ones are sealed by the sealing angel. The restraint is temporary. With frightful and fearful judgment ready to break out upon the Earth, it is necessary to secure the servants of God - to preserve them from the wrath of Satan that shall be poured out (Rev. 12:13-17).

Exactly what the seal really is in the forehead of those saved, cannot be asserted. It must be a contrast to the mark of the beast (Rev. 13:16, 17). It will be something that will guarantee ownership and security.

7:4-8 The Sealing of the 144,000 (The Remnant of Israel Sealed)

7:4

Here we have the record of the Lord preserving 144,000 of Israel during the Tribulation who will not bow their knee to the Antichrist. This sealing is not the sealing of the Holy Spirit, but it is the sealing at the hand of the Angels.

The 144,000 Israelites will be earthly Israel, the literal seed of Abraham, living at that time, and not of a mystical or spiritual Israel. Though the "Twelve Tribes" were long ago lost and integrated among the lost nations of the world and scattered among the Gentiles, their whereabouts is not unknown to God.

Already in our generation of these last days, the Hebrews are being restored into their land. I believe all of the twelve tribes are being assembled from the four corners of the Earth (Ezek. 37:15-22). Those who spiritualize the Scriptures, making Israel and the church one - and confessing law and grace, rob the nation of Israel of her promised blessings and in so doing commit a serious evil.

7:5-8

In the listing of the twelve tribes, there are several peculiarities to recognize.

1. The word for "seal" is repeated after each tribe. The Lord has put His seal upon them and no one is able to break this seal.

2. Judah heads the list, supplanting the tribe of Reuben, the first born, whose right to that position had been forfeited by Reuben's sin (Gen. 49:3, 4, 8-10).

3. The tribe of Dan and Ephraim are omitted from the list. Both of these tribes were guilty of going into idolatry (Deut. 29:18-21).

7:9-10 The Saved Gentiles (A Saved Multitude)

We learned from the first eight verses that there will be souls saved during the Tribulation, and that the first contingent will be the Jews. Here we meet another great multitude, but they are Gentiles. During this time of Gentile salvation the Church is with the Lord, having been caught up with Him. She is seen "sitting" around the throne (4:4). These "stand" before the throne and before the Lamb (7:9). The exact number is known only to God.

They are the Gentile converts won to the Messiah as the results of Israel's restoration. The prophet Isaiah wrote of them in Isa. 49:10.

I do not personally believe that this throng has in it any who reject Christ in this present dispensation. I believe those who deliberately reject the love of the Truth in this age are without hope in the coming age, based on II Thes. 2:10-12.

This throng heard the good news of the gospel of the kingdom for the first time through the 144,000 redeemed children of Israel. As a result a great multitude will be saved, most of them will by martyred, and will be raised at the close of the Tribulation period.

When the disciples asked our Lord what would be the sign of His coming at the end of the Age, He answered in Matt. 24:14. By "the end" I believe Christ meant the end of the Tribulation (Matt. 24:29; Dan. 7:1-25; 9:24-27). This throng will be preserved through the Tribulation, not kept out of it as the church will be.

7:9

The scene now is transferred from Earth to Heaven, for the multitude which he saw appeared, "before the throne of God in Heaven."

The size of this multitude is stupendous. These are Gentiles who have been saved during the Tribulation. These converts will come from every corner of the Earth. You will note in verse 15 the word "shall" is in future tense. Later on He shall come to this Earth and set up His kingdom and then those shall dwell upon the Earth and He shall dwell over them in perfect righteousness. They owe a debt of gratitude to those 144,000 Jewish missionaries, the wise who shall shine because they turned many to righteousness (Dan. 12:3).

The white robes symbolize the righteousness of Christ - made white in the blood of the Lamb. A difference may be observed, for verse 9 says that this white-robed throng have palms in their hands. The redeemed host in Heaven (Rev. 4:4) also had white robes but they were crowned and did not have palms. This company has palms, but are not crowned.

The palm is the only tree mentioned in the construction of the Millennial Temple (Ezek. chapters 40 and 41). It is also named briefly in connection with the Feast of the Tabernacle, the closing joyous feast of Israel (Lev. 23:40).

Palms are to express joy? They have gone through the sorrows of the Tribulation and their victory is now complete.

7:10

The countless multitude of these redeemed ones break out in one loud united cry of praise to God and to the Lamb for their salvation.

7:11-12 The Saying of the Angels
The Praise of the Heavenly Host

This is a stupendous scene of universal worship of God by His creatures. Notice they are praising God for His attributes and goodness, but not for salvation - they are sinless creatures and not redeemed sinners. Here is true worship indeed.

7:11

This picture is a picture of a series of great concentric circles of the inhabitants of Heaven. On the outer ring stand all the angels. Nearer the throne are the twenty-four elders; and still nearer are the four living creatures; and before the throne are the white-robed martyrs. The martyrs have just sung their shout of praise to God, and the angels take that song of praise and make it their own.

7:12

Here the heavenly company ascribe the blessing to God, and all God's creation must always be blessing Him for His goodness and His kindness in creation and in redemption and in providence to all that He has created.

Then the heavenly host ascribe Glory to God. God is the King of Kings and Lord of Lords, and to Him Glory must be given. God must be given the adoration and the glory which are His by right.

Then they ascribed Wisdom to God. God is the fountain of all wisdom and the source and origin of all truth. Our real wisdom can also come from Him (James 1:5).

They offer Thanksgiving to God. He is the giver of salvation and the constant provider of grace. He is the creator of the world and the constant provider of all that is in the world (I Thes. 5:18; Psa. 103:1-3).

Then the heavenly host ascribe Honor to God. It may be that sometimes we come unconsciously to think of God as someone to be used - someone out of whom we get things - someone to whom we continuously go with requests upon our lips. We do well not to forget the claims of worship, and bow ourselves humbly in the presence of God and offer honor to Him in everything.

They also ascribed Power to God. God's arm is never shortened and His power never grows less. There is no helplessness in God - He works His purpose throughout the ages.

Then they ascribed Strength to Him. To find the source of strength in life is extremely important (Phil. 4:13).

7:13-14 The Special Inquiry
The Elders Question and Answer

7:13

Who this elder is we do not know. Seemingly, this is the same one in Rev. 5:5 and told John not to weep when no one was worthy to open the book. Since John does not recognize this great host of people, then this group does not belong to the church. John would have recognized them. If they were Old Testament saints or Israelites, John would have known. These are the redeemed Gentiles, who have come out of the Great Tribulation, redeemed by Jesus Christ.

7:14

The word "out" in this verse is translated from the Greek word *ek*. It is the same word that is translated "from" in Rev. 3:10. That is, the church would be kept "totally from" the tribulation because they would be in Heaven while the tribulation was taking place. The martyrs here in chapter 7 are come "out of the Great Tribulation" - taken "totally out from" something they had been in. The church is kept out of the tribulation - the martyrs came out of the tribulation. There are actually three groups of believers mentioned in Revelation who will be saved during the Tribulation.

1. There is the remnant which is saved and martyred during the first half of the tribulation (Rev. 6:9-11).
2. There are the 144,000 Jews saved during the first half of the tribulation period and sealed by God for their protection.
3. There is the great "multitude," which no man could number who are saved during the last half of the Great Tribulation (Rev. 7:9 -14).

They were the garments of saints - they are attired in unspotted righteousness and faultless splendor, acquired through the Savior's blood. The white robes always stand for two things. They stand for purity, for a life totally cleansed from sin through Jesus Christ. They stand for victory, for the life that is victorious over sin.

7:15 The Service of God - Serving Him Day and Night

There is one very significant fact hidden here. The task of serving God day and night was part of the task of the Levites and priests (I Chron. 9:33). Now these who are before the throne of God in this vision are drawn from every race and tribe and people and tongue. Here, indeed, is a revolution. In the earthly Temple in Jerusalem no Gentile could enter in beyond the court of the Gentiles. To have done this would have been to become liable to death. An Israelite could enter further into the Temple. He could pass through the Court of the Women and enter into the Court of the Israelites - but beyond that not even an Israelite could go. Beyond that was the Court of Priests, and into that court no layman might enter. That court was for priests and priests alone.

But now there is no question of Jews or Gentiles; the way to the presence of God is open to people of every tongue and every race. There is no question of everyone having access to the inner presence of God.

One of the great blessings for the people of the Lord will be that He "shall dwell among them." The literal translation of this statement is, "shall spread His tabernacle over them." God, in the Old Testament, spread His tabernacle over the tent in the wilderness, which thus became the center and rest for thousands of Israelites. Two million people were sheltered from scorching suns and winter's blasts by the huge canopy which God spread over them - invisible but nonetheless real. It was the nations glory and defense.

In the eternal state (Isa. 4:5) the tabernacle of God is with men - the millennial times God's tabernacle will be over them. What a sense of security we shall enjoy as we bask under the glorious overspread canopy, each member of the countless throng equally sheltered, equally protected.

7:16-17 The Shepherd's Security (The Bliss of the Blessed)

The Lamb continues to feed and lead His own. These verses definitely identify the multitude as Tribulation Saints. During the reign of the Antichrist no one can buy or sell without having upon himself the mark of the beast. Those who refuse to receive the mark cannot buy or sell - those who receive it cannot be saved. Therefore, the saved people, having refused to receive the mark of the beast will be forced to hide out under the heat of the sun by day and the stars by night. Many times they will be hungry - destitute of food. They cannot buy food. Therefore, "they will not hunger any more, neither thirst any more" (Isa. 49:10).

Here is the promise of the loving care of the Divine Shepherd of His flock. The greatest title that the prophet can give to the Messianic King is to depict Him as the Shepherd of His people (Ezek. 34:23; Heb. 13:20).

The concluding statement in this chapter is that, "God shall wipe away all the tears from their eyes." These words are unequaled in their combined depth and tenderness. If He wipes away every tear, they shall never weep again (Rev. 21:4).

Revelation Chapter Eight

Following the interlude of chapter 7, the seventh and final seal was broken. There is only one short statement about it: "There was silence in Heaven for about half an hour." But, within the context of the book, this is a significant statement. It denotes the "calm before the storm." The two series of judgments which follow (the seven trumpets and the seven bowls) are of a severe nature, and they seem to be the actual content of the day of God's wrath.

The opening of the seventh seal produces the seven trumpets which announce the severe judgments during the Great Tribulation - the last three and a half years of the seven year period.

The judgments of the Tribulation now increase in their intensity. These judgments are not repetition of what has already gone before, but they are progressive in their intensity. The trumpets do not simply follow the seventh seal; they come out of the seventh seal. This is true also of the bowls of wrath which later come out of the seventh trumpet. Therefore, the three series of sevens are really included in the first seven seals. There is no overlapping but rather a progression in the intensity of judgment. Thus, out of the seventh seal comes a panoramic view of the last half of the Tribulation.

There is a definite parallel between the seven trumpets and the seven vials of chapter 15-16.

TRUMPETS	JUDGMENT	VIALS
1. 8:1-7	1. The Earth	1. 16:1-2
2. 8:8-9	2. The Sea	2. 16:3
3. 8:10-11	3. The Rivers	3. 16:4-7
4. 8:12-13	4. The Heavens	4. 16:8-9
5. 9:1-2	5. Mantino - Torment	5. 16:10-11
6. 9:13-21	6. Army - Euphrates	6. 16:12-16
7. 11:15-19	7. Nations in Wrath	7. 16:17-21

The four series of sevens can be explained in the following manner:

1. Seven Seals - judgment which is the result of man's willful activity.
2. Seven Trumpets - judgment which is the direct activity of God.
3. Seven Personalities - judgment which is the result of Satan's fight against God.
4. Seven Vials (Bowls) - final judgment of the Great Tribulation, which is the direct activity of God because of man's and Satan's rebellion.

8:1 The Silence in Heaven - Opening of the Seventh Seal

The Lord Jesus is still in command. When He opens the seventh seal, there is introduced a fanfare of seven trumpets. First of all He orders a halt on all fronts - Heaven, Hell and Earth. Nothing can move without His permission.

Now for a brief moment there is a lull in judgment activity. This is the lull before the storm (Isa. 28:21).

The seven-sealed book, or scroll, seen in the open hand of Jehovah (5:1-2) has its seals successively opened by the Lamb. In this verse He opens the final seal. But why is the seventh seal separated from the preceding six? Naturally one would suppose that it would have concluded Chapter 6. But instead, a whole chapter (chapter 7) comes in between the sixth and the seventh seal. The sixth seal announced judgment of such an appalling character that in the universal terror which ensued the fears of men, from king to slave, supposed the general horror to be the great day of wrath of the Lamb. But no, and so before the seventh seal is opened, which is preparatory to the infliction of yet further and more severe judgments, the veil is drawn aside to see two great companies from among Israel and the Gentiles are introduced on the scene.

The "silence in Heaven" which follows the opening of the seventh seal comes as a sudden surprise. Now the dramatic action is resumed. The seventh seal is opened. Then there followed a silence in Heaven.

If this silence in Heaven had been intended as a mere dramatic pause, even as such it would have heightened the effect and increased the eager curiosity as to what would follow. The impression of this surprising silence is tremendous.

The "silence in Heaven" is far more than a literary device. It is intended to show the structure of the book. The opening of the seventh seal is followed by a silence because the contents of the seventh seal are not to be revealed - not at once. This is the calm before the storm. The two series of judgments which follow (the seven trumpets and the seven bowls) were of a very severe nature.

This half an hour denotes a brief period, and a broken period. The word here used - *nuiopios* - does not occur elsewhere in the New Testament. It is correctly rendered "half an hour." This then, denotes a brief period of time. In a state, however, of anxious suspense, the moments seem to move slowly. The awfulness of the stillness itself makes this half-hour a thing so tremendous that we may be sure there never was the like before, and never will be again thereafter.

8:2 The Seven Angels - The Solemn Preparation

Note carefully the fact that the seven trumpets are a part of the seventh seal, and are not to be construed as another review of the judgments under the six seals.

We are introduced to seven angels who stand before God. This is a beautiful statement. It emphasizes that Christ is in complete charge of everything which takes place during the Tribulation.

These are special angels. That the angels to which he here refers are a distinguished and select number seems evident from the insertion of the definite article "The seven angels" - not just "seven angels." The "seven" are distinguished from the seven who pour out the Vials (15:1). Only of these trumpet angels is a special position ("before God") predicated.

Note also, there are seven of these angels - representing the full, complete power of God in judicial judgment.

There are distinctions amongst the angelic hosts. They are distributed into various orders and ranks, but all, from the archangel down to the least, are servants. They have no relationship to God founded on redemption. They are servants, and never rise out of that position, nor do they desire it.

They stand: this is the posture of service; but standing in the presence of God, is to be above all other servants (Esth. 1:4; Luke 1:19).

The seven angels received the trumpets, took their positions as directed and prepared to sound. This denotes a sovereign action, and the judgments which follow are not accidental. The trumpets are increasingly severe. The vials are very severe.

The seven trumpets before us tell of the great final intervention of God in judgment. These trumpets will not be calling men to work or worship. They are warlike in character and they tell us that divine judgment is about to fall upon the wicked ones who dwell on Earth.

8:3-5 The Saints Supplication
The Priestly Messenger

In this passage we see an angel officiating at the altar of incense in the heavenly sanctuary. That there is a Temple in Heaven is evident from difference passages (Psa. 11:4). We can see from these verses that there is a service conducted in Heaven. The one taking the leading part in it is called "an angel," and it is this angel who is officiating at the altar of the Holy Place.

8:3

In the Old Testament order the priests would burn incense upon the altar of incense, and the smoke would fill the Temple or the Tabernacle and then would ascend to Heaven. Incense was symbolic of worship and prayer and a reminder that intercession to the Lord has the character of sweet incense.

Now this points clearly to a Temple in Heaven. Connecting back with Rev. 7:17, we find the throne mentioned and also the temple in Rev. 7:15.

Now in Rev. 8:3 we find an altar before the throne which was not mentioned by John before. This indicates that in Heaven there is a temple built after the pattern of that which was revealed to Moses on the mount (Heb. 8:5; Ex. 25:1). The heavenly temple is mentioned again in Rev. 11:19, and it is evidently in Heaven until eternity begins; but when eternity begins and the New Jerusalem comes down from God out of Heaven (a city 1,200 miles square), this city no longer has any temple in it. The Lamb is the Temple thereof (Rev. 21:22).

It is only from Heb. 9:4 that we learn that the censor in use in the yearly day of atonement was of Gold. The censor was employed to carry the fire from off the brazen altar.

A large quantity of incense was here given to him, because the occasion was one on which many prayers might be expected to be offered. The idea is plain, that, when the prayers of the saints ascended, he would also burn the incense, that it might go up at the same moment, and be emblematic of them.

The incense employed in the tabernacle service of the Old Testament was composed of four ingredients specified in Ex. 30:34-36.

At the altar the messenger brings the prayers of the saints. These are, of course, the saints who are on Earth. The intercession of the saints in Heaven has already been turned into praise and adoration.

These "all saints" are the converts of the 144,000 sealed messengers of God (Rev. 7). They are a part of the great multitude which no man could number (Gentiles). They are praying because they are going through such suffering under the hand of the Antichrist.

8:4

The smoke of the incense came with the prayers of the saints and ascended up to God out of the angel's hand. The prayer in Rev. 6:9-11 is here being answered in Rev. 8.

8:5

The censor which has held incense for the worship of God is now filled with fire from the altar, and the fire is cast upon the Earth. There is no incense mixed with the fire. The incense and prayers went up to God, the fire was cast down upon the Earth. So we see the same altar brought salvation and judgment. Now the judgment of God falls upon those who reject the provision made on the cross through the Lord Jesus Christ.

The description of the voices, thundering, lightening and earthquakes will be real and literal. Number 4 is the world number and there are 4 judgments that fall upon the Earth.

8:6 The Sounding of the Seven Trumpets

This is a solemn moment. The half-hour of silence is over. The prayer of the saints have been heard. The order is issued to prepare to blow.

These seven angels do not themselves execute the judgments—they only announce them by the blast of the trumpet. When it is said that they "prepared themselves to sound". We are not to think of the mere mechanical functions of the act of sounding a trumpet, but of a deliberate adjustment among themselves of the place and subject which each one was to take in his work.

We thus have a very significant hint respecting angelic ministration, to wit: that the affairs of men and nations are much more under the influence of the thinking and deliberation of angels, and wear much more of the impress of angelic management, than we are accustomed to suppose.

8:7 The First Trumpet - Burnt Vegetation

As we study these trumpets, there are three major points which will be helpful to remember:

1. The series of trumpets is divided into two main groups: the first four trumpets are concerned with the realm of nature. The last three emphasize mainly the realm of the demonic or the heavenly.
2. Most of the destruction resulting from the first four trumpet judgments affect one-third of the objects involved—with a few exceptions. A third part has always symbolized judgment (Ezek. 5:2).
3. Each of the last three trumpets are called "woes". This seems to indicate the extreme character of these final judgments.

The day of wrath of the lamb has come. The first angel prepared to sound, and when he sounded there followed hail and fire mingled with blood. This is a fulfillment of Joel 2:30-31. No less than five of the nine plaques of Egypt are to be repeated during the tribulation period.

Hail is always used of judgment. The plague of hail in Egypt is but one example (Isa. 28:2; Job 38:22, 23). A mingling of fire and blood only adds to the violence and death of that hour.

We now witness the dire results produced by the manifest judgment of

Heaven. All plant life is included in the judgment of the first trumpet. In Gen. 1:11, 12 we are told that plant life was the first to be created after the heavens and Earth. And now the judgments of trumpets have first the destruction of plant life.

In turning away from God, man has turned to nature. So now in judgment, the Lord Jesus brings judgment on nature so man will see God is above all. This devastation will affect one-third of the earth's surface.

8:8-9

After the first angel or messenger announced his judgment on Earth, now the second messenger begins to fill his place of service.

The first thing to strike our attention is the little clause "as it were". Here is a definite indication of symbolism. The mountain is not a literal mountain. It looks like a mountain of fire that is cast into the sea (Hosea 4:3). In this day of nuclear fission, all of these things become more literally possible than we had ever thought.

When this great burning mass fell into the sea, it turned a third part of the sea into blood. This has already happened on a smaller scale in Egypt (Ex. 7:19-21).

You will note that a particular sea was mentioned. The word is singular. It is my belief that this is the Mediterranean Sea, around which the greatest recorded events of the world and of the church have been enacted. Also, one-third of the ships will be destroyed.

8:10-11 The Third Trumpet - Bitter Waters!

I believe this is a literal star or meteor that soars through space, approaching the Earth. In its sweep along the surface it turns one-third of earth's water into a deadly poison. The gaseous vapor that will be scattered by this meteor will be absorbed by the water—causing one-third of it to become deadly.

It will be well to note that thirteen times in chapter 8 the phrase "the third part" is used. Thirteen is the number of rebellion and evil and this reveals the judgment that comes because of rebellion against God.

Note these Scriptures: Jer. 9:14-15; Jer. 23:15. Wormwood is a perennial herb, very bitter, and is used in the manufacture of absinthe (a poisonous vermifuge—worm spray). The result of this embittering of the waters is fearful distress on account of the absence of wholesome drink, and great mortality among men.

It seems that this bitterness will continue until the establishing of the Millennial Kingdom (Ezek. 47:6-9).

8:12-13 The Fourth Trumpet - Beginning of Heavenly Judgments

Here is a prophecy, the fulfillment of which will baffle all scientists. These events were predicted clearly by Jesus in Luke 21:25-28. On the fourth day He brought the sun, moon and stars into view in order to provide light for men. Under the fourth trumpet He will take a part of that light away.

Here the scene changes from Earth to the celestial bodies. Once again one-third of the area was affected, so that one-third of the day and one-third of the night might not shine in their accustomed fashion. Thus, the Earth will be enveloped in total darkness at certain periods.

Then John saw and heard an angel (rather translated "eagle"). The eagle is used in the Old Testament as a symbol of God's judgment (Deut. 28:49; Hosea 8:1). This eagle speaks. If man can teach a parrot or parakeet to speak, I doubt God will have any trouble with an eagle. God didn't have any trouble teaching a donkey how to talk in Numbers 22.

Everyone will hear the message of the eagle. The repetition of the "Woe" is intensive. The remaining three trumpets will indicate great and fearful calamities.

Revelation Chapter Nine

And now the fifth messenger sounds and the trumpet and the first woe begins. A star is seen that has fallen to the Earth. In the last chapter we saw it in the course of it falling. The result was bitterness and wormwood. We now see it fallen to the Earth. I feel this star is a symbol of Satan himself.

When the fifth trumpet is sounded, swarms of locusts appear. They appear from the "pit of the abyss." These locusts are demonic creatures. They have the power to sting like scorpions. Instead of consuming vegetation, they attack men. As the Israelites were exempt from the plagues of Egypt, so these men escape who have "the seal of God on their foreheads."

9:1 The Unnamed Personality - The Fallen Star

In the original text, the words, "A star fall from Heaven" really reads, "The star which has fallen from Heaven." Notice that this star acts with intelligence. He is given a key which means he is given authority. It seems more accurate to interpret this star in Revelation 9 as Satan, because the star has already fallen, acts with intelligence, and is given authority.

In the middle of the Tribulation (Isa. 14:12, 15; Luke 10:18), as recorded in Rev. 12:7-12, Satan will be "cast out into the Earth." This ends his ability to accuse the brethren. The word "fall" is the perfect tense which signifies completed action. That this is Satan is verified in verse 11 when he is called "the angel of the bottomless pit."

To this personage is given the key to the bottomless pit, or pit of abyss. This is the first instance the original is translated "bottomless pit." The word is ABYSSAS. This is the abode of demons according to Luke 8:31 (deep = ABYSSAS). It is here that Satan himself is confined for a thousand years during the reign of Christ (20:1-3).

9:2 The Uncovered Pit - The Furnace Smoke

Reference to the abyss is found nine times in the New Testament and more than thirty times in the Bible. A careful study shows that it is a place in which are to be found beings which have come under the judgment of God (II Pet. 2:4; Jude 6).

This bottomless pit does not refer to Hell, because this is not opened until the Great White Throne Judgment (Rev. 19:20; 20:13, 15).

When this pit opened, a gigantic volcano belches forth its smoke until the sun and air are darkened. In this chapter there are more occurrences of the words "as" and "like" than in any other chapter of the Bible. This reveals how difficult it is to put this dreadful sight into human language. This smoke will completely black out the sun, and there will be darkness over all the land. This is a smog of the most vicious type.

9:3-6 The Unknown Punishment - Demonic Locusts

At first these demonic creatures which take the form of locusts are mingled with smoke, but when the smoke clears away, they appeared in great numbers. The appearance of these locusts are not ordinary because:

1. They will eat no vegetation (Ex. 10:3-20)
2. They have a king. Ordinary locusts do not (Prov. 30:27).
3. The description of them proves them to be different than average locusts.
4. They are not stifled by the smoke of the pit as ordinary locusts would be.
5. Ordinary locusts do not arise from the infernal regions.
6. They are not to torment the sealed Jews.

Scorpions are native to the Holy Land, with some species growing to six inches in length. They are used in the Bible as a symbol of painful judgment (Deut. 28:38, 42; I Kings 12:11-14).

Even though the locusts of Rev. 9 are not comparable to natural locusts, they are literal creatures. They are demons who take on the form of these unique locusts. When Satan invaded the Garden of Eden he came in the form of a serpent (Gen. 3:1). When Jesus commanded the unclean spirits to come out of the maniac of Gadara, they went into a herd of swine (Mark 5:12, 13).

9:4

The realm of their power to hurt and destroy is on the unsaved man. They were not to hurt the trees, grass, or any green thing. They dare not hurt men with the seal of God in their foreheads. These locusts will be limited in that they may not kill men, just torment them.

9:5

The plague of "locusts" upon mankind did not bring fatal results; rather, it was a five month period of torment, for they stung like scorpions. For five full months these demon locusts will stings and torment men.

9:6

Death is an enemy that had dogged the footsteps of lost mankind to this present moment. Due to the intensity of suffering during these five months, man will seek death, but cannot find it. These five months will seem like years.

9:7-10 The Underworld Persons - Description of Demon-Locusts

Note carefully the fluent use of "like" or "as" which makes this a simile of comparison. These beings are similar to, but not identical to, literal locusts. They are demon spirits who take on a form to torment men.

This is a detailed description of this demon-locust. It is frightful, weird and unnatural at first inspection. However, a closer examination of the text reveals a striking resemblance of the Palestinian locust.

The writer does not say that these were literal crowns actually made of gold. He says "as it were" crowns, etc. This probably was a gold circle around their heads as a feature of the creature.

These locusts have faces as faces of men - or, they had human countenance. This is another reason to know these are demonic beings. Satan has always tried to deceive men through bodies. He'll try to deceive men through our bodies if we permit it. That's why we need Rom. 12:1-2.

These creatures had long hair such as women usually wear (or did once upon a time). Their teeth were strong and sharp like a lion's teeth (Joel. 1:6).

The locust has a hard and firm cuticle on the forefront of the breast, which shields or serves as a defense while it moves through thorny and sticky vegetation. They also are equipped with wings which give forth the sound of many chariots going to battle (Joel 2:5). Many have commented on the weird and frightening sound the locust makes.

These locusts have tails like scorpions, and these tails have stingers in them. These creatures are given the power to hurt and sting men for five months.

9:11 The Unscrupulous Prince - Demonic Leader

The king over these demons is Satan, who is described in both Hebrew (*Abaddon*) and Greek (*Apollumi*). Both words mean "destroyer."

The name being in both Hebrew and Greek is an indication that the judgment will come upon both Jew and Gentile.

9:12 The Unanswered Period - Warning Announced

The word "woe" in Scripture refers to some great calamity (Matt. 11:21). Desperate indeed will be the situation of those who know not Christ in these tragic hours preceding His return to judge the wicked world.

9:13-15 Second Woe - Angels Loosed

When the fourth trumpet was sounded the apostle John heard an "angel flying through the midst of Heaven, saying with a loud voice, "Woe, woe, woe to the inhabitants of the Earth by reason of the other voices of the trumpet of the three angels, which are yet to sound" (8:13). This second woe has to do with supernatural warfare.

With the sounding of the sixth trumpet, John hears a voice described as coming from the four horns of the golden altar before God. The horns seems to indicate that the altar is similar to the design of the altar of incense used in the Tabernacle and in the Temple. Why was the voice not heard from the altar itself; instead of the four horns? In Rev. 16:7 the voice comes from the altar itself. Why, here, does the voice come from the four horns? All numbers in the Bible have spiritual significance. Four expresses world universality. It is the number of the world. The voice coming from the horns denotes power over all the universe.

9:14

These four angels are not the same as the four angels of Rev. 7:1. These four angels are bound in the great river Euphrates. The angels in chapter 7 hold back the forces of evil. The four angels here in chapter 9 let loose the human and satanic instruments of destruction and judgment. These are evil angels who are loosed to execute judgment. They probably are fallen angels who followed Lucifer in his rebellion and revolt against God (Isa. 14:12-14). Good angels are never bound, but are free to serve God. These angels are bound.

The beginning point is the "great river Euphrates," the place famed in ancient history as one of the earliest sites of civilization. From earliest times, Satan seems to have been connected with this region, for the river Euphrates had its source in Eden, the garden of temptation for Adam and Eve. Again in Rev. 16:12-14, Satan and his cohorts are seen in action at the Euphrates. The river Euphrates is 1,780 miles in length, and is by far the most important river in Western Asia.

9:15

The period of time is not indicated here, as is evident by the omission of the article and preposition with day, month and year. One the basis that the article is used only before the word hour in the Greek construction, it should be translated "the hour, and day, and month, and year." The interpretation being "the appointed hour occurring in the appointed day, and in the appointed month, and in the appointed year." The time schedule is determined by God, not man, and even angels execute God's will in God's time.

The mission of these angels is to slay one-third of the inhabitants of the Earth. This brings the whole world into the sphere of divine operation. One of the purposes that the Lord has in sending the Tribulation upon the world is to destroy all the wicked out of it in order that He might establish a reign of righteousness.

What a catastrophe it will be when the four angels slay the third part of men? The fourth of the world's population who died with the opening of the fourth seal and the third who are slain by the four angels in the judgment of the sixth trumpet total half the world's population destroyed in these two judgments. This does not count all who die from the plagues during the Tribulation.

9:16-19 The Unrestrained Power - The Army of Death

The moment the four bound angels are released from their constraint, hosts of death-dealing cavalry overrun the Earth. There are such things as supernatural horses. (Horses of fire took up Elizah into Heaven). Heavenly horses and horsemen introduce the dominion of Christ, as described in a later chapter in this book. These horses are the powers of the four loosed angels, inbreathed with the spirit of death and destruction and putting into execution their murderous and malignant will. As there are infernal locusts, so there are infernal horses; and as the former were let forth to overrun the world with their torments under the fifth trumpet, so the latter are let forth to overrun the world with still more terrible inflictions under the sixth.

9:16

This is an army of 200 million. This is a supernatural army, but it is not of God. We must always remember that everything supernatural is not necessarily of God. This is a demonic army. This immense host is a number too vast for human conception. Yet, in this vision in Revelation there is no difficulty in understanding the number. If a legion of demons could possess the Gadarian demonic (and a legion is 6,000 persons), then 200 million might be but a small part of the "spiritual hosts of wickedness in the heavenly (atmospheric) places" (Eph. 6:12).

9:17

John also gives a graphic description of the horses as well as of the warriors who sit upon them. They are declared to have breastplates of fire and of jacinth and brimstone. Fire and brimstone are symbols of destruction and punishment (Gen. 19:24).

While they were weapons of Hell, they are nevertheless the emblems of God's judgment. Brimstone is a gas with a sulfurous smell. It was this stifling and strangling gas that God sent upon Sodom when He destroyed it (Luke 17:29). The coming judgment of Babylon will take on a similar form (Rev. 14:10), as will the judgment against the beast and the false prophet (Rev. 19:20), Satan (Rev. 20:10), and eventually all unbelievers (Rev. 21:8).

The writer does not say they were heads of lions, or that the riders were on monsters, but only that they resembled the head of lions. Out of their mouth issued fire, and smoke and the brimstone will do the work of slaughter. The "third part of man" will be slain. The horsemen do not do the killing - they have only defensive weapons - the horses do the slaying.

9:19

These unnatural horses are able to kill with their mouths. The weirdest feat of all is that, instead of hair for a tail, they have serpents which also are used in destroying mankind.

There was something remarkable about these creatures that John had noticed. That is the position and appearance of their heads. All serpents, of course, have heads, but John saw something unusual in this. It would seem most probable that the heads of these serpents appeared to extend in every direction - as if the hairs of the horses' tails had been turned into snakes, presenting a most fearful and destructive image.

9:20-21 The Unrepentant People - Result of Judgment

The two closing verses of this chapter reveal an astounding picture of human depravity. These people see the awful doom of their fellow associates, but it makes only a passing impression. They fail to repent.

9:20

The death of approximately one billion people on the Earth, with the accompanying grief and the confusion which must follow such a disaster, finds the residue of people not willing to repent. Such is the human heart! Here Satan is at his best in the hearts of men.

More people will "worship devils" than ever before. This type of worship is much on the increase today. Churches of Satan are springing up all over the country.

Here in this verse we are able to see the state of society in the days of Antichrist. Demon worship is rampant. Those who remain do not repent of their demon worship, their worship of idols of gold, silver, brass, stone and wood. Many of these tendencies are very visible in our day. Works always follow doctrine and are developed from it. A man becomes what he believes. Those who are false in creed are false in character. The bad state of the society of that day is seen by the pit into which the population sinks after the judgment of the sixth trumpet passes.

9:21

Capital punishment will be totally suspended in my thinking and murder will become rampant. How is it going today? During that day man's life will be filled with murder, sorcery, fornication and stealing.

The word which we here have translated "sorceries" is in the original *pharmakeia* - from which we get our word pharmacy. It comes from a root which means drugs. This probably refers to the craving-habit forming addition which destroys a person's will. Drug addiction will become even more widespread than now. It will be one of the means the Antichrist will employ to make the population subservient to his will.

Society will be deluged with the sins of fornication and adultery, the institution of sacred wedlock will be denounced and the teaching of free love will prevail. We're headed in that direction now!

The last crime in the category is theft. This is a statement of general and abounding dishonesty, the obliteration of moral distinctions, the disregard of others' rights, and the practice of fraud, theft, and deceit wherever it is possible. In our day corruption in high places gives the example to all classes. The only wrong consists in getting caught.

Revelation Chapter Ten

Parenthetical Section 10:1 - 11:14

Between the breaking of the sixth and seventh seals there is a parenthetical period covered by chapter seven of Revelation. Between the sounding of the sixth and seventh trumpets there is another parenthetical section of 10:1 - 11:14. In the first parenthesis we see the sealing of the 144,000 and the effect of their ministry; in the second parenthesis we see the death, resurrection and translation of the two witnesses and a description of the effect of their ministry.

This chapter introduces us to the middle of the tribulation period. According to Dan. 9:27, this is the time the Beast breaks his covenant with Israel and reveals himself in his satanic fury. Note also that the two witnesses minister during the first 3 1/2 years (11:3); the Jewish remnant is protected by God during the last 3 1/2 years (12:6, 14); the Beast has worldwide authority the last 3 1/2 years (13:5); Satan is cast to Earth for 3 1/2 years of awful persecution against the believers (12:2); and Jerusalem is trodden down of the Gentiles for 3 1/2 years (11:2).

10:1 The Appearance of the Mighty Messenger

The messenger here is characterized as a "mighty" angel - one of strength and power; implying that the work to be done by His mission demands the interposition of one of great power and leadership. Let us look at seven things that probably give us His identity.

1. This Angel is mighty - powerful - possesses great strength.
2. This Angel came down from Heaven.
3. This Angel is clothed with a cloud.
4. This Angel had a face like the sun.
5. The feet of the Angel are as pillars of fire.
6. He has in His hand a "little book opened."
7. He stands with one foot on the land and one on the sea - denoting universal ownership and authority (Psa. 24:1)!

These seven facts testify that the Angel could be none other than the

Lord Jesus, in my opinion. The first appearance of this one is in 7:2. The second appearance is in 8:5. In the first instance He acts as Prophet. In the second He acts as Priest. In this passage He acts as King.

This graphic description of the Angel of Jehovah takes us back to the Old Testament days, for we feel the cloud with which He is clothed is the Shekinah Glory (Isa. 6:1-8; John 12:41; Acts 1:9).

In this verse we see a rainbow upon the head of the Mighty Messenger. We know the rainbow is the symbol of God's everlasting covenant with the Earth (Gen. 9:12-13), therefore, we would not expect any one but the Divine Christ to wear it upon His head (Ezek. 1:28). This is one of the four times the rainbow is mentioned in God's Word, and on every occasion it is connected with God's mercy given unto men. The rainbow is a sign of God's mercy, not angelic mercy.

The face of this one was like the sun. In Rev. 1:16 John saw the countenance of Jesus "as the sun shining in full strength." Jesus is referred to in the Bible as "the Sun of Righteousness."

His feet were as pillars of fire. The same statement is made of the feet of Jesus in Rev. 1:15. Nothing like that has been said about any ordinary angel - not even to Michael or Gabriel, the archangels.

10:2 The Action of the Mighty Minister

The messenger holds in his hands a small scroll that is unrolled. Commentators differ widely as to the significance of the scroll. This is the same book mentioned in chapter 5, when John "wept much" because no one could be found worthy to open the book. But, one was found - the Lion of the tribe of Judah, the Lord Jesus Christ. Here in our present Scripture the book is open and the Mighty Messenger is holding it in His hand. He stands with one foot upon the land and the other foot upon the sea. The book is now opened and judgments are on display. With the title deed of this Earth in his hand, and by placing his right foot on the sea and his left foot upon the Earth, in a great voice he claims all for Heaven (Lev. 25:23; Psa. 8:6-8). The book is described here as a little book because the time of the Great Tribulation is short (Rom. 9:28).

Here we see the little book contains the judgments by which Christ uses His power and authority to take over the Earth. He wrests the control away from the devil and takes possession for Himself as the rightful Heir.

Satan will assert his claim to the Earth, but when Christ "puts His foot down" He will take possession of His own property.

10:3-4

This is the voice of the Lion of the Tribe of Judah. It is a cry of power and victory. The cry was an announcement of vengeance upon the enemies of God and the wicked who at that time will inherit the Earth (Joel 3:16; Jer. 25:29-31). The shout from the Mighty Messenger is the announcement of the immediate oncoming judgment of God, and Heaven answers in seven thunderous voices.

Thunder is a recognized type of God's voice in judgment (I Sam. 7:10; Psa. 18:13). The number seven is suggestive of the completeness and finality of the Mighty Messenger's sayings (Psa. 29; John 12:28-29).

The prophet was about to record the words of the thunders. John understood what he heard. But, there were two commands given to John: first, to seal up the sayings of the thunder; second, to write them not. No indication of the correct interpretation of the seven thunders is given. Sadly, some commentators have tried to do what John was forbidden to do.

10:5-7 The Announcement of the Marvelous Message

Here we turn from blood, strife, chaos, demon maniacs, Antichrist to God's eternal purpose concerning the Earth.

This verse presents a magnificent picture. The Mighty Messenger with all the brightness of the sun, all the roaring fire of a furnace about His feet. The clouds of glory compose His robe and compass His body. The brilliance of the rainbow makes up His diadem. There He stands - one foot on the land and one on the sea. The wide extended Earth and the mighty oceans serve as His footstool as His flaming feet stand to conquer and possess. With His mighty hand raised up to Heaven, He speaks and vast regions of the firmament echo with His mighty voice.

This Mighty Messenger (Jesus), now speaks an oath as an appeal to God. The word "swear" here means "calling upon a person or power to witness to the veracity of a statement with the added incentive of punishment if the statement is not true." This is not to be confused with cursing. The oath of this Messenger not only assures us that the judgment of God is not going to be delayed any longer but guarantees the immediate execution of it.

He who created the Heaven, the Earth and all that there is therein is the One who shall bring this judgment upon mankind (Col. 1:16).

The actual rendering of the statement "that there should be time no longer" should read, "that there should be no more delay of time." The souls under the altar in Rev. 6:10 had asked a question. The answer was given in 6:11. Now the Lord states that there will be no more delay. When the seventh messenger sounds his trumpet, the mystery of God will be finished.

Several things should be noted in connection with verse 7:

1. The voice of the seventh messenger is heard for some considerable time. "In the days of the voice."
2. The completion of the mystery is to take place "when he is about to sound."
3. The completion of the mystery is something that has been declared by God through the prophets.

When the Mighty Messenger asserts His righteousness over this Earth, the program of God will reach its completion without delay.

Here we must not confuse the coming judgment of God with the mysteries of Christ. The secret here in Revelation refers to what had already been made known by God to the Old Testament prophets. The great secrets concerning Christ and His Church were confined to the New Testament.

1. The mystery of God's will (Eph. 1:9, 5:32, 6:19).
2. The mystery of iniquity (II Thes. 2:7).
3. The mystery of godliness (I Tim. 3:16).
4. The mystery of God (Col. 2:2).
5. The mystery of the seven stars (Rev. 1:20).
6. The mystery of the Rapture (I Cor. 15:51; I Thes. 4:13-18).
7. The mystery of Israel (Rom. 11:25).

The mystery mentioned in Rev. 10:7 will be unfolded at the time when Jesus Christ will stand with the Earth and the sea under His feet, and His hand raised toward God's throne.

Jesus Christ will wrest the governments of Earth out of the hands of Antichrist and take over the governments of Earth Himself (Isa. 9:6; Luke 1:32, 33). Jesus will personally put the devil on the chain gang for one thousand years. Then Jesus will reign with His Bride here on Earth for one thousand years, and then after the Great White Throne, Jesus will reign forever (Isa. 9:6, 7).

10:8-10 The Appropriation of the Manuscript

After the utterance of the Angel, John hears the voice from Heaven apparently to be identified with the same voice he heard in Rev. 4:1. John is commanded to take the book previously described. This little book is the same seven-sealed book described in chapter five. Now it is opened and its contents ready to be revealed. John was commanded to go and take the little book out of the hand of the Messenger - and he obeyed immediately.

In obedience to the command of the voice, John goes to the angel and requests that he be given the little book. The instruction was, "Take it, and eat it up; and it shall make thy belly bitter, but it shall be in thy mouth sweet as honey" (Ezek. 3:1, 3, 14). To John, the roll was sweet and bitter at one and the same time. What he means is this: A message of God may be to a servant of God at once a sweet and bitter thing. It is sweet because it is a great thing to receive a message from God. But, the message itself may be a message of warning, therefore the message is bitter. Sweetness and bitterness were intermingled in the task of being the messenger of God.

I believe the prophecies of coming judgment leave the child of God with great heaviness of heart and bitter anguish of soul (Rom. 9:1-3). God's Word is a two-edged sword. It contains the sweet message of salvation and deliverance and the bitter message of damnation. He who appropriates the Book cannot escape the mixture of sweet and bitter.

10:11 The Assignment of Ministering to Multitudes

We must bear in mind that these chapters which we are now studying portray to us the events which will take place after the rapture of the church; that God will then be dealing once more with Israel as a nation; that the age of grace will have ended with the taking away of the church; and the Jew, not the Gentile, will occupy the center of the stage. The last verse of chapter 10 leads us immediately into new phases of God's fury and judgment.

Revelation Chapter Eleven

The chapter before us is admittedly a difficult one. If you have read it for yourself, it is obvious that conclusions cannot be arrived at hastily. Much prayer and study has to go into the interpretation of this chapter.

The guiding lines which this writer used to govern the exposition regard this chapter as a legitimate prophetic utterance in which the terms are taken normally. Chapter 11 of the Revelation continues the parenthetical section beginning in chapter 10 and extending through chapter 14. With the exception of 11:15-19, introducing the seventh trumpet, the narrative does not advance in these chapters and various topics are presented. In chapter 15, the chronological developments continue as the contents of the seven trumpets, namely the seven vials are manifested.

This chapter brings us to an economy much like Old Testament times. The temple, time periods, and the distinction between Jesus and Gentiles indicate that there is now an Old Testament type of economy.

Also, note the conclusion of the interlude between the sixth and seventh trumpets and the blowing of the seventh trumpet. It is interesting to note that this chapter opens with the temple on Earth and closes with the temple in Heaven. The temple on Earth is the Tribulation Temple. The temple in Heaven is the original from which Moses received the blueprint to make a tabernacle in the wilderness (Ex. 25:40; Heb. 8:25, 9:23, 24).

Chronologically the seventh trumpet brings us to the return of Christ at the end of the Great Tribulation. The Return of Christ is presented in detail in chapter 19. There is the open Heaven, here it is the open temple. Between chapters 11 and 19 many details of the Great Tribulation are given which would otherwise be unknown. Great personalities and nations that play a large part in this period will be given in detail beginning with chapter 12.

The temple in Jerusalem had been destroyed when John wrote this. He makes it clear that another temple will be built (the Tribulation Temple) - which will be a total rejection of Jesus Christ. The Tribulation Temple will finally culminate in the worship of an image of Antichrist.

Revelation 11 describes the beginning of the last three and one-half years of Great Tribulation. During this time the Gentiles will make their last strong attempt to frustrate God's plan and purpose. The "times of the Gentiles" will come to an everlasting end when Jesus comes in power and great glory and destroys the Antichrist and his armies. The account of this battle is found in Rev. 19:11-21.

At this point some important time notations are introduced (11:2, 3; 12:6, 14; 13:5). These seem to designate the same length of time. The average month during that day (lunar year) was regarded as thirty days. Forty-two months is equal to 1,260 days, the latter expression also defining the "time, and times, and half a time," equaling three and one-half years (Dan. 7:25).

Jerusalem will be trodden under foot by nations (Gentiles) for forty-two months (Luke 21:24-27). Actually this is the period that designates the last half of the Great Tribulation.

11:1-2 The Temple is Measured

We observe at once that the language is peculiarly Jewish. This whole chapter is looking to the rebuilt temple in Jerusalem during the Tribulation. None of this has been fulfilled up to this point in time.

In the opening verse of chapter 11, John is given a reed compared to a rod. This reed is native to the Jordon valley, and because of its light weight it constitutes a good measuring rod. John is instructed to measure the Temple of God, the altar, and them that worship therein. This instrument was usually ten feet long (Ezek. 40:3; Zech. 1:16).

Up to this point John has been a spectator on the scene. Now he becomes a participant. The angel instructed him to "rise and measure." The act of measuring was a characteristic action of taking possession. Jesus is now ready to take possession of the temple and He has it measured to see if its functions meet His qualifications. The Lord makes known the fact that the Temple and all its services and worshippers are not coming up to the standards that are acceptable to God. The measuring reveals the deficiency and failure of the worshippers.

This temple will be built in the "holy city" - or Jerusalem. Here a magnificent temple will be erected and many worshippers will gather. In that temple the personal Antichrist will appear and claim the right to be worshipped (II Thes. 2:4). This is the abomination of desolation spoken by Daniel (Dan. 9:2) and attested by Jesus (Matt. 24:15).

The court which is outside the inner temple is to be left out. The followers of the Antichrist have profaned it and they shall be allowed to trample it under foot for 42 months. This is obviously the last half of the Great Tribulation.

11:3-12 The Two Witness Ministers

In this time of treading down, God has reserved to Himself His faithful witnesses. The number is small - just two - but it is sufficient, for in the mouth of two witnesses every case shall be established (II Cor. 13:1).

These two witnesses are to testify for a certain period and we read that when they had completed their testimony the beast that ascends out of the bottomless pit shall make war against them and overcome them.

The burden of the message of the two witnesses will be one of judgment. That is why they are clothed in sackcloth. They have no rank or dignity upon Earth, though it is declared that they stand in the presence of the Lord of the Earth.

The two witnesses are called "two olive trees" and "two candlesticks." The question arises, "who are the two witnesses?" There are two schools of thought on this matter that we will pursue.

There are those who believe these two witnesses to be Moses and Elijah. It is suggested that the number "two" is symbolic and stands for the unity of two representatives who come in the spirit of Moses and Elijah. These witnesses have miraculous power given them. They have power to bring drought, to turn water into blood, and to smite the Earth with plagues.

They note that Elijah brought drought to Israel and Moses was connected with the plagues of Egypt, which included the Nile being turned into blood.

Others believe that the two witnesses are just men raised up of that day to serve the Lord in this capacity.

11:3 These Witnesses are Persons

It was always a part of Jewish belief that God would send His special messenger to men before the final Day of the Lord (Mal. 3:1; 4:5). This seems to make it clear that Elijah will be one of the messengers. This being true, it is no trouble to accept the other being Moses. There is an interesting line of thought in connection with the bodies of these two men. Elijah did not die (II Kings 2:9-11). The death and burial of Moses holds a secret (Deut. 34:5, 6; Jude 9). We must at least consider the possibility that Michael was commissioned by God to secure the body of Moses and to be kept in some way by God for the fulfillment of His purpose. It is interesting to note that Peter recognized Moses and Elijah on the Mount of Transfiguration.

The days of their testimony are carefully numbered. The number of months is forty-two - six times the period that ark was in captivity. Six is the number of evil, and weakness; and seven of completion, and these two numbers (6 and 7) are the factors of 42; which seems to signify a fullness or completion of the weakness in these months.

Sackcloth is worn as a mark of sorrow and grief. It will suggest extreme bitterness of soul. They will be prophesying the terrors of the Lord.

11:4 They are Prophets

These two witnesses are described as two olive trees and two lampstands who stand before the God of the Earth. This seems to be a reference to Zech. 4:6. The olive oil from the olive trees in Zechariah's image provided fuel for two lampstands. The two witnesses of this period of Israel's history (Joshua and Zerubbabel), were the leaders of Israel in Zechariah's time. Just as these two witnesses were raised up to be lampstands or witnesses for God and were empowered by olive oil representing the power of the Holy Spirit, so the two witnesses of Revelation 11 will likewise execute their prophetic office. Thus we see that the phrase "two olive trees" is explained by Scripture to mean two persons.

11:5-6 They are Powerful

These verses record the miraculous powers given to the two witnesses. Anyone trying to hurt them will be destroyed by fire proceeding out of their mouths. This is at once a judgment of God upon their enemies and a measure of protection for the two witnesses, so that no one can lay a hand on them. See II Kings 1 and Numbers 16:35.

The text implies that there would be those who would be disposed to injure or wrong them - that is, they would be liable to persecution. The word "will" is better translated "intends" or "purposes." I can make nothing of the record but to take it literally. I find no difficulty in this. The horsemen were supernatural beings from Hell, and the two witnesses are supernatural beings from Heaven.

These two witnesses not only have power and command to kill with fire, but otherwise to torment and afflict the wicked world. They have power to shut Heaven that it not rain during the days of their prophecy. They also have power to turn water to blood at their will, and to smite the Earth with plagues. They are delegated this authority to exercise this power "as often as they will." This reveals the confidence that God places in these faithful servants (Psa. 37:4, 5).

We often harbor too much pity for Satan and his enemies. What about Christ and His church? How about a little pity for the two witnesses for Christ? God's protective hand is and will be on His own - He will not permit them to be harmed until their ministry is finished.

11:7-10 They are Persecuted

The fact that the beast is able to kill the two witnesses proves they are mortal beings. They are killed by a person - not a movement.

As in the case of many other great prophets of God, when their ministry is finished, God permits their enemies to overcome them. None other than Satan himself makes war against them and kills them. I believe that God's servants are always invulnerable against the onslaught of the enemy until their work is done.

The question is often asked, "why did God not translate them if their work was done?" May I suggest two reasons:

1. God desired to give them the martyr's crown. This is one of the greatest things He could do for them.
2. God desired to set forth the villainy of Earth's people.

God knew what was in men, but He wanted us to know. Now the true colors of men reveal themselves.

These two great saints are not even accorded a decent burial. This reveals the crude, cold barbarism of the last days. They are treated as dead animals.

So significant will be the testimony of the two witnesses that their death at the hands of the beast shall cause an international stir. Notice the place where they die - "the holy city" (11:2). Note carefully the Holy Spirit is to tell us that the city is spiritually, not literally, Sodom and Egypt. Jerusalem is not literally Sodom, but spiritually is likened unto the old city (Isa. 1:9, 10; Deut. 32:30-33; Jer. 23:14). Jerusalem is spiritually like Egypt because of its gross idolatry (Ezek. 23:3-19). The statement "where also our Lord was crucified" identifies the city as Jerusalem.

Apparently a television camera will play upon their features for three days and a half (v. 9). The morbid curiosity of a godless society will relish the opportunity of gazing with awe upon their dead bodies. It was a Jewish tragedy not to be buried (Psa. 79:2-3).

Why would they lie in the streets three and one half days? The Jews believed that the Spirit of a dead man hovers nears the body for three days. That is why Jesus waited until the fourth day to go to the tomb of Lazarus. The Jews would not have acclaimed it a miracle had it been during the first three days. In the case of the witnesses, the Lord wanted them to know that their resurrection was a miracle.

Their death is an occasion for great rejoicing. They even send gifts to one another all over the world. Television and satellites will make the fact of their death known around the world within minutes. They will have merry feasts and exchange gifts as if it were Christmas. These people are happy to be rid of their "tormentors." A righteous prophet is always a torment to a wicked generation.

11:11-14 They are Preserved

The merrymaking of those who rejoice in the death of the two witnesses is cut short after three and one-half days by the witnesses' restoration to life. As they stand on their feet before the startled gaze of those who watch, it is recorded that great fear falls upon those who see them. Their amazement increases as they hear a voice from Heaven saying to the witness, "come up hither."

Think of it! During the three days and one half, exposed to the heat of the sun and the elements, the dead bodies were already decaying. Then, suddenly, and without warning, they stood upon their feet. This reminds us of Lazarus in John chapter 11.

These two witnesses are then ushered into the presence of God in a cloud of the shekinah glory while all the world watches. For at least one fear-filled moment, the world will realize that there is a greater power than the Antichrist.

At this point there is a great earthquake in the city of Jerusalem. One-tenth of the city is destroyed and seven thousand men are destroyed. "The remnant" better translated "the rest" - those who are not killed, become terrified and out of fear acknowledge the God of Heaven. This doesn't mean they were converted, but shows they finally recognize the power of God (Phil. 2:10-11).

11:15-19 The Announcement of the End. The Seventh Trumpet - Blessing in Heaven

We are now about ready to see Rev. 10:7 come to pass.

11:15

This passage is difficult in that it seems to indicate that things have come to an end in final victory, while yet half of the book is left. The explanation is that this passage is a summary of all that is still to come. The events that are foreshadowed here are as follows:

1. There is the victory in which the kingdoms of the world become the kingdoms of the Lord and of His anointed one, the victory which is the beginning of His eternal reign.
2. This victory leads to the time when God takes His supreme authority (v. 17). It leads to the thousand-year reign of

> Christ - the Millennium. The Millennium is a thousand year period of prosperity and peace.

The kingdoms of this world are presently under Satan's rule. Jesus said He is "the prince of this world." This "one-world" system man is trying to bring in through the United Nations, and other ways, is of Satan. It becomes more godless and wicked every day. It is a condemned civilization.

The fact that the earthly rule will pass into the hands of God is frequently mentioned in Old Testament prophecy (Ezek. 21:26-27); Dan. 2:35; 44; Zech. 14:9). With the seven vials still to be poured out, how can this be now at the sounding of the seventh trumpet? Just as the seven trumpets are comprehended in the seventh seal, so the seven vials are comprehended in the seventh trumpet.

The phrase "and He shall reign for ever and ever" is an all-inclusive term which encompasses the Millennial reign, the final rebellion, the Great White Throne Judgment and the eternal state.

11:16-17 The Acclaim of the King

The elders begin to worship when they see through to the end. Note that they see:

1. The kingdoms of the world become the kingdom of the Lord and His Christ (11:5 — compare 19:20; Psa. 2:8).
2. The universal reign of Christ (11:5 — compare 20:4-6).
3. The angry nations (11:18 — compare Psa. 2:1-3).
4. They see the resurrection of the wicked dead (11:18 — compare 20:11-15).
5. They see the reward given to prophets and the saints, both Old Testament and New Testament believers (11:18 — compare Luke 19:11-19).
6. They see the temple of God and the ark of the covenant (11:19). This may be the "last look." In the New Jerusalem there will be no temple (21:22). In the millennial age it would seem that the ark of the covenant will not be known (Jer. 3:12-17).
7. They see the final physical manifestations of lightning and earthquakes attended by voices of thundering (11:19). This

final earthquake is referred to in Zech. 14:4 when the Lord Jesus returns to the Mount of Olives.

These elders fall on their faces in worship and rejoicing in the prosperity and final triumph of the Lord. The second chorus begins by thanking the Lord God, the Almighty, who inhabits eternity (Isa. 57:15). God's throne is exalted above all and His authority is over the entire universe (Psa. 103:19-22; Psa. 62:11).

Now these elders praise God because He takes His great power and reigns. This statement harmonizes with the thought in verse 15.

11:18 The Anger of the Nations - Wrath is Displayed

In contrast to the worship of the twenty four elders is the anger of the nations. This anger grows in its intensity until finally they openly declare war against the God in Heaven, and think they can overcome Him (Rev. 19:19).

This verse is a general statement teaching that in general it is time of divine wrath, a time of resurrection of the dead and their reward, and a time of special dealing with those living on Earth. All of these aspects of the second coming of Christ are borne out in later prophecies in the book of Revelation.

The reward given to the prophets and saints, as well as those who fear the name of God, is a reward of Old Testament saints. The church had already been raptured to Heaven before the Tribulation began. The saints of the Church Age are represented in Heaven by the twenty four elders while the Tribulation is raging on Earth. These elders are seen wearing white raiment with crowns of gold on their heads (4:4).

This verse also emphasizes that the time has come for God to "destroy them which destroy the Earth." This includes both man and Satan. Judgment comes when Christ returns to Earth at the end of the Tribulation.

11:19

After the pronouncement of the great voices in Heaven saying that the time of God's wrath has come, John sees the temple of God in Heaven. This chapter opens and closes with the temple.

What is the significance of the "ark of his covenant or testament?" It means that God has not forgotten His covenant which He made unto Abraham, Isaac and Jacob. As the end of the tribulation draws to a close, God will let us see the fulfillment of every word He has ever promised.

This heavenly temple is the pattern after which the Jewish temple was patterned (Ex. 25:40; Heb. 9:23). The fact that John sees the temple of God and the ark indicates that Israel is coming into view and that God will once more renew His dealings with Israel nationally.

There are five names given to the Ark in the Old Testament.

1. "Ark of the Covenant" - because it contained the two tables of law (the old covenant) (Num. 10:33).
2. "Ark of testimony" (Ex. 25:22).
3. "Ark of God" (I Sam. 3:3).
4. "Ark of God's Strength" (Psa. 132:8).
5. "Holy Ark" (II Chron. 35:3).

In the latter part of verse 19 there appears a terrific storm (Rev. 4:5; Rev. 8:5; 11:19; 16:18).

Revelation Chapter Twelve

"The Conflict in Heaven and Earth"

In Chapter 12 through 14 of Revelation, the great actors of the tribulation time are introduced. This is another parenthetical section ending at 14:20. These great actors or personages are seven in number:

1. The woman (representing Israel).
2. The dragon (representing Satan).
3. The man-child (referring to Christ).
4. Michael (representing the angels).
5. Israel (the remnant of the seed of the woman).
6. The beast out of the sea (a world dictator).
7. The beast out of the Earth (the false prophet and religious leader of the world).

What a sweep of prophecy we see in this short section. From the birth of Christ (12:5), to His treading the winepress of God's wrath (14:20).

12:1-2 The First Great Wonder, The Woman Clothed with the Sun: Israel

12:1

The "great wonder" in Heaven could be better translated the great "sign" *(semeion).* This is a sign or symbol of an important truth - not just a wonder. There are seven "signs" or miracles in Revelation:

1. 12:1	3. 13:13-14	5. 16:14
2. 12:3	4. 15:1	6. 19:20

Though the sign is seen in Heaven, it is portraying a reality on Earth, for subsequently the woman pictured is persecuted by Satan in the great tribulation.

The woman is described as clothed with the sun, having the moon under her feet, and on her head a crown of twelve stars. Further, she is waiting the imminent birth of her Son. The identification of the woman as Israel seems to be supported by all evidence. The twelve stars represent the twelve tribes. Her persecution coincides with Israel's persecution.

There are four representative women in the Revelation:

1. Jezebel (2:20) - Corrupt religious system.
2. The woman in authority (12:1) - Israel.
3. The great harlot (17:1) - The corrupt, apostate church.
4. The Bride (19:7) - The church glorified in Heaven.

12:2
The child here represents Christ - that is to be delivered. The translation of "to be delivered" could be translated "after being delivered" (Isa. 66:7; Micah 5:2, 3).

12:3-4 THE GREAT RED DRAGON: SATAN (DAN. 7:7-8, 24)
There is a double view in mind here. The dragon is called Satan in 12:9, but the description seems to indicate that it is Satan as he is fully represented in the revised Roman Empire. The color red indicates his murderous characteristics. The seven heads and the ten horns refer to the original ten kingdoms of which three were subdued by the little horn of Dan. 7:8.

The tail of the dragon is declared to draw a third part of the stars out of Heaven and cast them to Earth. This may refer to the gathering under his power those who oppose him politically and spiritually involving his temporary subjugation of a large portion of the Earth.

The reference to the dragon awaiting the birth of the child with the intent to destroy it as soon as it is born unmistakably alludes to the circumstances surrounding Christ's birth, and the attempt of Herod to destroy Jesus. (Note that Herod was an Edomite as a descendant of Esau - traditional enemies of Jacob.)

12:5-6 The Man-Child: Christ

12:5
The woman brings forth a man-child that is destined to rule all nations,

but who for the time being is caught up to God's throne (see Psa. 2 and Psa. 8). We have already stated that we believe the man-child to be Christ. To those who think it's the church, I suggest that (*hyan arsen*) "man-child" is masculine gender. If it were the church, it would be feminine gender. This man-child will eventually rule with a rod of iron (Rev. 19:15). His rule over all nations with a rod of iron is to be distinguished from His rule over Israel which is of more benevolent character (Luke 1:32-33).

The "catching up" of the man-child to God and His throne refers to His ascension. The word "caught up" (*harpazo)* is the same one used in I Thes. 4:17; II Cor. 12:2, 4 and Acts 8:39 (Luke 24:50).

12:6

Please note that there is a thirty-three year lapse between "brought forth" and "caught up" in verse 5. Now we have the whole history of Christianity between verse 5 and verse 6. This verse and verse 14 are the same, with verse 7 through 13 giving the reason for the flight. There in the wilderness Israel remains in a place God prepared for her for 1,260 days - exactly three and one-half years (Jer. 30:6-7; Matt. 24:15-28). God not only provides a place for them, but nourishment likewise.

12:7-9 War in Heaven - Satan Cast Out of Heaven

12:7

Though the conflict of the end of the age is primarily on Earth, attention is directed to the war which will be waged in Heaven. That Satan would have access to the throne of God in any way is difficult for most of us, but there must be an acceptance of the Word of God (Dan. 12:1; Job chapter 1; Isa. 24:21).

Who is Michael ("who is like God")? He is named five times in Scripture (Dan. 10:13, 21; 12:1; Jude 9; Rev. 12:7).

He seems to be the leader of the angelic hierarchy, as he is termed by Jude. In every occasion where he is named, the Jewish people are in question. It is my feeling that he is the chief angel to whose guardian care and interest of Israel are committed.

Here we see the war waging between Satan (v. 9) and his forces and

Michael and his forces. The title "devil" is from the Greek word "diabolos" meaning "defaming," or "slandering." He is the master accuser of the brethren. The name "Satan" has the meaning "adversary."

12:8

The dragon personally suffered on ignominious defeat, while the whole company of sinful angelic intelligence is for ever banished from "the Heaven." I believe that it is at this point that Satan turns his baffled rage against the woman (Israel), which ushers in the last three and one-half years of the Tribulation.

There seems to be three stages to the judgment of Satan:

1. He is cast down to Earth with his angels (Rev. 12:9).
2. He is confined as a prisoner in the abyss for one thousand years (Rev. 20:3).
3. He is consigned to eternal torment in the lake of fire (Rev. 20:10).

12:9

In this verse the special work of Satan is next stated. He "deceives the whole world." Satan himself is the leader in luring on the world to its moral ruin. The threefold repetition of the verb "cast out" is meant to emphasize the ignominious expulsion of Satan and his angels from Heaven. Eventually the heavens and the Earth will all be cleared of evil.

12:10-12 Announcement of the Coming Day of Satan's Wrath and the Ultimate Victory of the Saints

12:10

The salvation mentioned as now impeding refers not to salvation from the guilt of sin, but in the sense of deliverance and completion of God's divine program. The reference to strength implies that now God is going to strengthen His own and manifest His own strength. The "Kingdom of our God" refers to the millennial kingdom when Christ will reign on Earth.

The "brethren" in this verse are the same as the overcomers in verse 11 - the Tribulation Saints.

12:11

These saints overcome the accuser three ways:

1. By the blood of the Lamb. This renders the believer pure and makes possible his spiritual victory.
2. The word of their testimony. This opposed the work of Satan by presenting the Gospel as the power of God for salvation.
3. They loved not their lives unto the death. That is, they did not regard their own lives more precious than the message of Salvation. What about you and me?

12:12

The voice from Heaven continues to exhort the listeners, especially those in the heavens, to rejoice because of the great victory. At the same time the voice pronounces a solemn woe upon the inhabitants of the Earth and the sea. The awfulness of the hour ahead is attributed to the fact the devil has been cast into the Earth and has great wrath because he knows his hour of confinement is near. The word for "wrath" here is *thymos*, meaning "a strong emotion." This awful hour is caused by an emotional rather than a rational state of mind and stems from his awareness that his days are numbered. The "short time" is the last forty-two months of the Tribulation.

12:13-16 The Persecution of Israel in the Great Tribulation

12:13

The immediate aftermath of Satan's being cast out of Heaven is his persecution of the woman which brought forth the man-child. This is the beginning of the Great Tribulation of which Christ warned Israel in Matt. 24:15-22. Israel is hated by Satan not because of any of its own characteristics but because she is the chosen of God and essential to the overall purpose of God for time and eternity.

12:14

Into this scene of satanic persecution is injected the divine intervention of God. The woman is described as being given two wings of a great eagle in order to enable her to fly into the wilderness into her place. This figure of speech seems to be derived from Ex. 19:4 and Deut. 32:11-12 where God uses the strength of an eagle to illustrate His faithfulness in caring for Israel. This verse implies that there is supernatural care for Israel during this period. It is also clear that God will preserve a Godly remnant out of this group, but according to Zech. 13:8, two-thirds of Israel in the land will perish.

The time element of Israel's suffering is described as "a time, and times, and half a time." This is a reference to the final three and one-half years of the Tribulation.

12:15-16

The persecution mentioned as "a flood of water out of the serpents' mouth" probably refers to every means Satan uses to try to exterminate the nation. The terrain in that area makes the prediction a literal flood very improbable. Satan strives with all his power to exterminate the people of Israel. By divine intervention, both natural and supernatural means are used to thwart the program and to carry a remnant of Israel through to safety.

12:17

This verse states that the dragon is especially angry with those within the nation Israel who "keep the commandments of God, and have the testimony of Jesus Christ." There is a double antagonism against those in Israel who turn to Christ as their Messiah and Savior in these critical days. Undoubtedly many of them will suffer a martyr's death, but others will survive, including the 144,000 sealed in chapter seven.

Taken as a whole, chapter 12 is a fitting introduction to the important revelations given in chapter 13. Here are the principal actors of the Great Tribulation with the historic background which provides so much additional information. Israel, Satan, Christ, the archangel, and the godly remnant figure largely in the closing scenes of the age. Next the two principal human actors are introduced: the beast out of the sea and the beast out of the Earth, the human instruments which Satan uses to direct his program during the Great Tribulation.

Revelation Chapter Thirteen

The victory of Michael over the dragon resulted in the complete overthrow of Satan's power and influence in the heavens. Now that the dragon has been cast to Earth, the Earth becomes the scene of satanic operation. God-fearing Jews and Gentiles become the special objects of Satan's murderous hatred. His two principal ministers are before us in this chapter. Satan is the mastermind who works in and through these apostates. The first beast is a Gentile, characterized by brute force. The second beast is a Jew, characterized by subtle influence. This passage is first of all a revelation of the revived Roman Empire in its period of worldwide dominion, but more especially this paragraph directs attention to the evil character who exercises satanic power as the world dictator.

13:1-10 The First Beast: Historical Revival of the Roman Empire

13:1-2 The Emergence of the Beast Out of the Sea

13:1

The "I stood" probably refers to John standing upon the sand of the sea. The "sands of the sea" upon which the Seer stood symbolizes vast multitudes of people (Rev. 20:8). The Beast is without doubt the ancient Roman Empire reappearing on the scene (Dan. 7:7-8). For more than 1400 years the Roman Empire has not existed. Today we see the revival of that empire in the World Trade Organization.

The beast is described as having "ten horns and seven heads, and upon his horns ten diadems." The monstrosity of seven heads and ten horns refer to seven major nations that finally emerge in the confederacy as leaders, while the authority of the other three is seen just as a figurehead (Dan. 7:8). The ten crowns are the symbols of governmental authority.

The "names of blasphemy" denote their blasphemous opposition to God and to Christ (v. 6).

13:2

The Beast is further represented as "like to a leopard, and his feet as of a bear, and his mouth as a lion's mouth." This represents power (lion), strength and tenacity (bear), and swiftness (leopard).

Satanic power is given to this beast to make havoc as he sees fit. He is given Satan's own seat (throne) from which to operate.

13:3 The Deadly Wound of the Beast

Obviously one of the powers will be politically slain during this time of the tribulation, but the miraculous recovery of this power in the revised Roman Empire will be a miracle of wonder. The whole will be amazed at the power of the revised Empire to restore this fallen power to it previous strength.

13:4 The Worship of the Dragon and the Beast

Now Satan becomes the object of universal worship. Here is a scene wholly given up to Satan. In the eyes of men the dragon has just done what it was supposed God alone could do - given supreme authority to the Beast. Now the beast is also worshipped. The revised Roman character that exceeds anything ever before witnessed. What a horrible blasphemy - Satan worship - but, it is on the increase today. There will not be a worship of the triune God in that day (Father - Son - Holy Spirit), but a worship of triune Satan (devil - beast - Man of Sin). It may be that the battles of Ezek. 38 and 39, predicting the destruction of the northern confederacy, takes place just before this, thereby removing the threat of eastern and northern powers to this authority and reign.

13:5-6 The Blasphemous Character of the Beast (Dan. 7:8, 11, 25)

This beast is given power to blaspheme and boast for forty-two months (3 1/2 years). This is one of the main features of the Beast's kingdom - not just an incidental sideline. God and all His in Earth and Heaven, are openly railed upon and spoken against.

13:7 The Universal Dominion of the Beast

As anticipated in Dan. 7:23 where the beast devours "the whole Earth," here the worldwide extent of his power is indicated. "It was given to him" refers to the satanic origin of his power. Acting as Satan's tool, the beast is able to wage war against the saints throughout the globe - and to overcome them (Dan. 7:25; 9:27; 12:10). Many believers in Christ among both Jews and Gentiles perish as martyrs during the awful time of trial, while others are preserved in spite of all the beast can do.

The universal authority of the beast over the entire Earth is stated specifically in verse 7. The original text reads, "power was given to him over every tribe and people and tongue and nation." World conquest is now for the first time realized completely and is a satanic counterfeit of Christ's millennial reign permitted by God in this final display of the evil of Satan and wicked humanity.

13:8 The Universal Worship of the Beast

The entire world with the exception of the saints will worship the beast. Those who do not worship the beast are described as having their names written in the Book of Life (Rev. 3:5; 17:8; 20:12; 21:27; 22:19; Luke 10:20; Phil. 4:3). My position is that all names are in this book - and only those who trust Christ remain - the rest are blotted out (Rev. 3:5).

13:9-10 A Call and a Warning

The desire to have all Christian churches unite, or to unite all the religions of the world, has been advanced as a desired goal. Many are trying to accomplish this fact today. During the Great Tribulation a world religion will be advanced which will have as its focal point the worship of a man chosen and empowered by Satan himself. In that day, true believers of Christ will be separate from this world religion and will be the object of its fearful persecution.

The call to "let him hear" is very significant. The call to "hear" in this context also concludes the exercise of spiritual understanding. This exhortation is shorter than those given to the seven churches (Rev. 2:3). The clause "what the Spirit saith unto the churches" is here omitted. This is another evidence that the churches are no longer in existence during the time of tribulation. They have already been raptured out of the world.

Verse 10 carries with it a twofold meaning. First, the saints are not to resist and fight against the persecution of the Beast. Their weapons are not carnal but spiritual. This is the only way they can triumph. Their victories are moral and spiritual, not physical. Secondly, those who persecute the saints and lead them into captivity must in turn suffer the righteous wrath of God (Gen. 9:6; Matt. 5:28: Rom. 12:9; Gal. 6:7).

13:11-12 The Second Beast

After the revelation of the first beast, John now sees another beast coming up out of the Earth and occupying a secondary role supporting the activities of the first beast. Let us contrast these two beasts which John sees.

The First Beast	The Second Beast
1. Come out of an unsettled state of things - the sea.	1. Come out of a settled and established condition of civil and political government - the Earth.
2. A secular power.	2. A religious power.
3. Ten horns.	3. Two horns.
4. All powerful.	4. Subordinate to the first beast.

The second beast as having two horns like a lamb, but speaks like a dragon. This picture, among other things, supports the idea that this beast is religious in nature, but is motivated by the power of Satan (the dragon).

Evidence points to the conclusion that the second beast is the head of the apostate church. With a rise of the first beast to a place of worldwide dominion, the apostate church is destroyed (Rev. 17:16), and the worship of the whole world is directed to the beast out of the sea. The second beast survives the destruction of the apostate church, and he assists the beast in making the whole world worship him (the first beast).

13:13-14 The Deceptive Miracles of the False Prophet

The first miracle accomplished by the false prophet is described as a great wonder. The frequent use of *pieo* in the present tense seems to indicate repeated action, of which fire coming down from Heaven in the sight of men is an illustration. The Scriptures indicate the devil does have the power to do miracles and that by their use he deceives people into worshipping the beast.

The deceptive power of the beast is mentioned specifically in verse 14. By means of this power he performs miracles in the sight of the first beast. On the basis of the power and the impression it makes upon men, the second beast urges them to make an image of the first beast, described for the third time in this chapter as one who had been wounded by the sword and did live. This probably refers to the decline of the old historic Roman Empire and its revival. Note the words "did live." Though the Scriptures do not say so, it is apparent that the suggestion is followed through, and the image becomes the center of false worship of the world ruler. This image is mentioned seven more times in the book of Revelation (14:9, 11; 15:2; 16:2; 19:20; 20:4).

13:15-17 All Required to Worship the Beast

The word "life" in verse 15 is an unfortunate translation. The Greek word here is *pneuma*, which is commonly translated "breath." The word for "life" as we know it is *zoe*. To give real "life" to the image would be a prerogative of God alone. A more correct approach would seem to be that the image was made to have a "breath" (*pneoma*) of speech come it that made it seem human. This power of speech will be speech demonically controlled in order to turn humanity to a worship of the first beast as their god. Those who will not worship the beast will be sentenced to be killed.

The regulation is issued that all classes (no one will escape) of people who worship the beast are to receive a mark in their right hand or in their foreheads and that possession of this identification is necessary to buy and sell. The mark varies in that it is on the right hand of some and in the foreheads of others. In some cases the mark is the name of the beast and in others it is the number of his name.

The necessities of life, obtained by legitimate trading, will be denied those who, in faithfulness to God, refuse allegiance to the Beast. Social ostracism and death are the appointed portion of all faithful to God in this most awful crisis of human history. Combination is the order of the day. Religion demands it, the political world demands it, wealth and capitol demand it and labor demands it. All are working to one great end, Satan's fusion of all religious parties under the Antichrist, and all political and social parties under the Beast.

(It may be well to consider the proposal by the World Committee on Food to create a worldwide food surplus to be used in times of famine).

The name of the beast is withheld from us, but the number of the beast is given.

13:18 The Number of the Beast

We have already studied that number six is the number of man (see notes on Biblical Numeries). As the number 7 denotes perfection and completeness, 6 being short of that implies human imperfection and toil. The number 666 is an increase in moral significance, until man will witness open and direct opposition of God.

Revelation Chapter Fourteen

"The Victory of the Lamb and His Followers"

The point at which we have arrived in these apocalyptic visions is a most sad one. Truth has fallen in the streets; the blood of God's saints is shed like water; open defiance of God and proud boasting are witnessed and heard - good is almost banished from the Earth; and faith in God is almost gone. Now is heard the oft-repeated cry to Jehovah of the Jewish remnant, suffering more than all others under an accumulated load of distress. Now we are to be shown in a series of events the hand of God. There are seven distinct subjects in chapter fourteen:

1. The Lamb and the 144,000 on Mount Zion (14:1-5).
2. The angel with the everlasting gospel (14:6-7).
3. Prophecy of the coming fall of Babylon (14:8).
4. The doom of the worshippers of the beast (14:9-11).
5. The blessing of the saints (14:12-13).
6. The judgment of the son of man (14:14-16).
7. The angel with the sharp sickle (14:17-20).

14:1-5 The Lamb and the 144,000 on Mt. Zion

The translation of "a Lamb" is unfortunate. The original text indicates "The Lamb" (Jesus) is the personage in verse 1. There are many contrary views as to the identification of the 144,000 in this chapter. After much study, I feel the preferable view is that the 144,000 in this chapter are the same as in chapter 7. In their first mention they are seen in the beginning of the tribulation. In their second mention (chapter 14), they are seen still intact, preserved by God through the fearful days of persecution and standing triumphantly with the Lamb on Mt. Zion at the beginning of the Millennial reign.

Also, the best manuscripts of the original text indicate that the expression "having his Father's name written in their foreheads" should be "having his name and the name of His father written on their foreheads." By this expression they are clearly identified as belonging to both the

Father and the Son. This is a description in more detail of the "seal of God" mentioned in chapter 7. As Seiss points out in his book The Apocalypse, their identification with the Father is the mark of being saved Jews; their identification with the Lamb reveals their salvation through faith in Christ; their position on Mt. Zion a place of security, blessing, and glory in the earthly Jerusalem in the millennial Kingdom.

In verse 2, a new facet of the vision is given to John as he records hearing a voice from Heaven. The voice is described in majestic terms as being the sound of many waters and comparable to the sound of great thunder. John also hears the voices of harpers harping with their harps (lyres).

They are described as singing a new song of praise. Chronologically, the song John hears is their hymn of praise in Heaven during the time of the Great Tribulation, but the same song is echoed by the 144,000 who stand triumphantly on Mt. Zion after the tribulation. As is true of the rest of the vision in this chapter, the chronological order is not maintained, but rather different subjects are brought into view pertaining to the general theme of the ultimate triumph of God.

Also, John describes them as "not defiled with women for they are virgins." I feel there is a twofold interpretation involved here:

1. Necessary abstinence from marriage in the critical days of the tribulation when a normal marital life for a person true to God is impossible.
2. Spiritual purity. They are not defiled by love of the world or compromise with evil, but keep themselves pure in a world situation which is morally filthy. In like manner Israel is referred to frequently in the Bible as "the virgin daughter of Zion" (II Kings 19:21; Isa. 37:22; Lam. 2:13), and as "virgin of Israel" (Jer. 18:13; 31:4, 21; Amos 5:2).

The possibility that their virgin character signifies their spiritual purity is indicated in the next statement describing them as those "which follow the Lamb whithersoever he goeth."

The term "firstfruits" seems to refer to the beginning of a great harvest. The 144,000 are the Godly nucleus of Israel which is the token of the redemption of the nation and the glory of Israel which is to unfold in the kingdom.

The description of the 144,000 closes with the statement that they are without guile and without fault. In saying that they have no guile (*pseuoos*), the thought is that there is no falsehood or especially no false religion in them (see *pseuoos* in Rom. 1:25; Rev. 21:27; 22:15). They are also described as "without fault" - or, blameless and without stain in contrast to those who are apostates.

14:6-7 The Angel with the Everlasting Gospel

The next phase of the vision given to John in this chapter introduces "another angel" flying in "mid-Heaven" having the everlasting gospel to preach to the entire world. This "another angel" seems to be in addition to the seven angels introduced in 8:2, 8:3 and 10:1. The remaining portion of this chapter presents a sevenfold division consisting of the appearance of six angels including a vision of the Son of man between two groups of three angels.

The expression "the everlasting gospel" here is without the article "the" in the original text - making it just "everlasting gospel." Immediately we would conclude that it is the gospel message of salvation. However, in verse 7 the content of the message is quite otherwise, for it is an announcement of the hour of judgment of God and the command to worship Him. The "everlasting gospel" seems to be neither the "gospel of grace" that we preach today nor the "gospel of the kingdom," but rather the good news that God at last is about to deal with the world in righteousness and establish His authority and sovereignty over the world. Throughout eternity God will continue to manifest Himself in grace toward the saints and in punishment toward the wicked.

14:8 Prophecy of the Coming Fall of Babylon

The second angel appears and proclaims the fall of Babylon the great. Prophetically, "Babylon" sometimes refers to a literal city, sometimes to a religious system, sometimes to a political system, all stemming from the evil character of historic Babylon. Remembering that chapters 12-14 are an overview of all that is to come to pass from the middle to the end of the tribulation, with chapters 15-18 filling in details - then the context seems to lend itself to the destruction of actual Babylon (which may be a reference to Rome). This really comes at the close of the tribulation, making this announcement prophetic in form. The nations who participate in the spiritual corruption induced by Babylon ultimately share her divine condemnation and judgment.

14:9-11 The Doom of the Worshippers of the Beast

The third angel adds immediately to the pronouncement of the previous angel by proclaiming with a loud voice the doom of those who worship the beast. Anyone who receives the mark of the beast as required in 13:17 shall also partake of the judgment of God. It is described in most dramatic terms as wine that is unmixed, that is, untempered by the mercy and grace of God. They are declared to be "tormented with fire and brimstone in the presence of the holy angels, and in the presence of the Lamb."

This torment is to be "in the presence of the holy angels and the Lamb." This does not mean that the "presence" is the same location, but the presence means a "witnessing presence." The holy angels had been witnesses from their place on high of the horrible wickedness of the Beast. Now they will witness God's vengeance on the wicked ones.

14:12-13 The Blessing of the Saints

14:12

The word "patience" could be better translated "endurance" (II Cor. 1:6). In the state of things the saints can only hold fast and hold on. Death awaits them, but better to be killed by the beast than to be tormented with the beast. The saints are described as those who "keep the commandments of God, and the faith of Jesus Christ." Here is the proper link between works and faith so necessary for all ages.

14:13

Four times previously there is a record of a voice from Heaven (10:4, 8; 11:12; 14:2). Again in 18:4 and 21:3 a voice is heard, a direct communication from God as contrasted with communication through an angel. The reference to the blessing of those who die in the Lord from this time on is not a general reference to all saints who die, but specifically to those who die in this period, that is, as martyrs of the faith. It is far better to be dead at the hand of the beast than to have favor as his worshipper. This is followed by the expression, "Yea, saith the Spirit." The implication is that the voice from Heaven is none other than the voice of the Holy Spirit. Those who die in the Lord are described as resting from their labors with the rewards of their work following them. This verse is the second beatitude in Revelation (1:3; 14:13; 16:15; 19:9; 20:6; 22:7, 14).

14:14-16 The Judgment of the Son of Man

Judicial judgment is about to sweep the guilty Earth with the hand of destruction and clear it of evil. The harvest and the vintage are the familiar figures employed to express God's closing dealings.

14:14

The "white cloud" here symbolizes divine presence (Rev. 10:1; Matt. 17:5; Ezek. 10:4). Christ is said to come "in a cloud" (Luke 21:27), and "on a cloud" (Matt. 24:30), both meaning relatively the same thing. It is under the title "Like the Son of Man" that Christ with the state of things on the Earth, and judges the ungodly. The golden crown upon his head speaks of His glorified state and His royal dignity. The sharp sickle indicates this is the time of harvest, referring to the climatic judgment relating to the second coming.

14:15

As John beholds the vision of the Son of Man having a sharp sickle, he sees another angel come out of the Temple crying to the Son of Man to thrust in His sickle and reap, declaring that the harvest of the Earth is ripe. The holy angel is entreating Christ as the Son of Man in His position a judge of men (John 5:22, 27). The angel urges judgment at this time because, in God's sovereign plan as made known to the angel, it is time for judgment. The verb form in the Greek for "is ripe" (*exeranthe*) meaning "to become dry or withered" has a bad connotation (Matt. 21:19-20; Mark 3:1, 3; 11:20; Luke 8:6). The picture here is of a fruit or vegetable that has become so ripe that it begins to dry up and wither. The rotten moral condition of the world is dealt with now with a sharp sickle.

14:16

The results are instantaneous, but that is in vision only. This is only a vision of what is about to take place on the Earth. The details of this reaping will be unfolded in the Scriptures that follow.

14:17-20 The Angel with the Sharp Sickle

14:17

The use of angels to assist in the harvest of the Earth is now stated explicitly in verse 17. Though not enumerated, the angel of verse 17 is the fifth to appear in this chapter, and he comes from the Temple in Heaven. He also has a sharp sickle, indicating severe judgment.

14:18

Another angel comes from beneath the altar to exhort the angel with the sickle to begin his harvest. This is the sixth angel listed in this chapter. This angel comes from the altar to answer the prayer of the saints in Rev. 6:10. This angel has power over fire. This seems to indicate that the angel is acting in response to the prayers of the saints for divine judgment on the wickedness in the earthly scene with a purging judgment of fire of which he is capable. Here the picture is given as clusters of grapes on the vine that are fully ripe. The expression "fully ripe" (*ekmasan*) is a different expression from the harvest of verse 15. Though the figure is somewhat different, the spiritual meaning is the same. The time has come for the final harvest. Here the vine is producing the fruit of wickedness and corruption.

14:19

This vision of the angel, in response to the entreating, thrusting his sickle into the Earth and harvesting its vintage, casting it into "the great winepress of the wrath of God," is actually fulfilled in Rev. 19:15.

14:20

Jerusalem is the city to which this reference refers. As the judgment of God is being trodden out in "the winepress of God's wrath," the destruction will be so great that blood will run as deep as horses bits for 1,600 furlongs (200 miles). Such a vast destruction of human life in a circumscribed area has never been known in human history.

Revelation Chapter Fifteen

"The Vision of the Seven Last Plagues"

Chapter 15 and 16 of Revelation bring to a consummation the chronologically ordered events leading up to the second coming of Christ described in chapter 19. These are introduced in this chapter as the "seven last plagues" which are the divine judgments preceding the second coming of Christ. The chronological order of events in Revelation is presented basically in the seven seals (6:1-17; 18:1). The seventh seal includes all of the seven trumpets (8:1-9, 21; 11:15-19). The seven vials or bowls of divine judgment are included in the seventh trumpet. The second coming of Christ follows this order of events immediately after the seventh vial. The parenthetical sections (10:1-11:14; 13-14; chapters 17-19) do not advance the narrative chronologically. Chapter 19 of Revelation follows immediately after chapter 16 in chronological development.

15:1-2 The Sign of the Seven Angels with the Plagues

The final series of the seven last plagues is introduced by the vision in which John sees "another sign in Heaven." The word "another" refers to the two proceeding signs of chapter 12; 12:1 "a great sign in Heaven," and 12:3 the "great red dragon." These three signs taken together represent important elements in the prophetic scene.

1. Israel (the woman).
2. The final world empire under the control of the dragon (Satan).
3. The seven angels having the last plagues.

The sign in Heaven is described as "great and marvelous" (*mega bai thaumaston*). The words appear together only here and in verse 3 in the entire New Testament.

Central in the vision given to John are seven angels, apparently another group of seven angels not to be confused with any other group of seven, as the definite article is not used with this expression. These angels are described as having the seven last plagues. It is most significant that they are described as "last" most emphatic in Greek (literally: "having seven plagues, the last ones"). That they are the last plagues shows that they are the final judgments proceeding the second coming of Christ.

The seven plagues are further described as acts of judgment which "fill up the wrath of God." The concept of "fill up" means to bring to conclusion or to the ultimate goal. The wrath of God is the final expression of divine righteousness.

The scene in Heaven is described "as it were a sea of glass mingled with fire." This seems to be a reference to the same situation as in 4:6. Here the sea of glass has two variations. The sea of glass is said to be "mingled with fire." In both cases it is obvious that John does not see an ordinary sea because the heavenly hosts stand upon it. The symbolism is rich. The sea is designed to reflect the glory of God. In chapter 4 its description "like unto crystal" speaks of the holiness of God. Here the sea mingled with fire speaks of divine judgment proceeding from the holiness of God. The fact that the saints are able to stand upon it reflects the faithfulness of God in upholding His own in keeping with His divine character.

Upon the sea stand an innumerable company of those who "had gotten the victory over the beast, and over his image, and over his mark, and over the number of his name." These unmistakably are the martyred dead that are destroyed by the beast of Rev. 13:1-10. Their resurrection and reward are described in Rev. 20:4-6. They are also described as having "the harps (lyres) of God."

15:3-4 The Song of Moses and the Song of the Lamb

The hymn of praise sung by the martyred saints in glory is identified as "the song of Moses the servant of God, and the song of the Lamb." The definite article in both cases would lead to the conclusion that two songs are in view rather than one. The former recounts the faithfulness of God to Israel as a nation in recognition that a large number of Israelites are among those martyred dead. The song of the Lamb speaks of redemption from sin made possible by the sacrifice of the Lamb of God, and would include all saints.

I personally believe the "song of Moses" is a reference to Deut. 32, a song personally written and spoken to the children of Israel by Moses at the close of his career. It is a comprehensive picture of God's faithfulness to Israel and His ultimate purpose to defeat their enemies.

Most of verse 3 and 4 is a passage of praise and honor to the Lord. The prospect of all nations worshipping the Lord, a familiar theme of the prophets, is brought out in the final two statements of verse 4 (Psa. 2:8-9; 24:1-10; 66:1-4; 72:8-11; 86:9; Isa. 2:2-4; 9:6-7; 66:18-23; Dan. 7:14; Zeph. 2:11; Zech. 14:9).

15:5-6 The Tabernacle of the Testimony in Heaven Opened

Here our attention is arrested by the phrase "I looked, and beheld." This expression always introduces something dramatically new. As John observes, the Holy of Holies in the heavenly Tabernacle is opened. It is described as "the tabernacle of the testimony" because of the presence of the tables of stone containing the ten commandments which were placed in the ark of the testimony in the Holy of Holies.

As John looks intently on the scene, the sanctuary is opened (the curtain is parted) and seven angels are seen coming out of the sanctuary. Each of the angels is carrying one of the vials containing the seven plagues and is described as being clothed in pure white linen and girded with a golden girdle.

The whole scene is most symbolic of what is about to happen. The angels coming out of the sanctuary indicate that the judgments of God that are poured out stem from the holiness of God who must do all things right. Linen here, as in the garments of the wife of the Lamb (19:8), represent righteousness in action.

15:7-8 Seven Golden Vials Given to the Angels

The seven angels described as already having the seven plagues in verse 6 are given seven golden vials or bowls described as full of the wrath of God. The bestowal of the authorization to use the plagues is symbolized by the bowls. The word "full" indicates the devastating character of this divine judgment.

As the angels emerge from the sanctuary, it is filled with smoke proceeding from the Glory of God and His power, a pointed reminder of the ineffable holiness of God. Access into the sanctuary is made impossible by the smoke until the judgment contained in the seven plagues are fulfilled. It is an ominous sign of impending doom for those who persist in their blasphemous disregard of the sovereignty and holiness of God.

Revelation Chapter Sixteen

"The Vials of the Wrath of God"

16:1 "The Command to Pour Out the Vials"

The "great voice" that commands to pour out their divine judgment upon the Earth is undoubtedly the voice of God. The term "great" (*megales*) occurs several times in this chapter.

1. "great heat" (v. 9)
2. "great river Euphrates" (v.12)
3. "great day of God" (v. 14)
4. "great earthquake" (v. 18)
5. "great city" (v. 19).
6. "great Babylon" (v. 19)
7. "great hail" (v. 21)
8. "great plague" (v. 21)

There is undoubtedly much similarity between the trumpet judgments and the judgments inflicted by pouring out of the vials of the wrath of God. Yet, a careful study of the seven vials as compared to the seven trumpets will reveal numerous differences. That is why I reject the idea that the vials are only an enlargement upon the trumpet judgments. The first four trumpet judgments deal with only one-third of the Earth, while the vial judgments seem to be universal in their application and greater in intensity. It is my position that the vial judgments are subsequent to the trumpet judgments and proceed out of and constitute the seventh trumpet.

16:2 The First Vial

There is a noticeable contrast between the first vial and the first trumpet. The first trumpet (8:7) burns up a third part of the trees and all the green grass. Here the judgment is specifically upon men and is directed to a particular group of men, namely, the beast worshippers who have received the mark of the beast. The judgment is described as a sore or ulcer (*helkos*) which is "noisome" (bad) - (*kakos*), and grievous (malignant) - (*poneros*). The judgment is in the form of physical affliction of unusual severity bringing widespread suffering.

Confirmation that the vial judgments occur late in the Great Tribulation is given in the record that the first vial judgment falls on those who are worshippers of the beast's image. The image is established during the early part of the final 3 1/2 years of the tribulation. Almost everyone seems to comply with the demand that all men worship the beast and receive his mark. The vial judgment, therefore, follows this edict. The warning given in 14:9-11 is now reinforced in preliminary judgment which anticipates the ultimate doom of the beast worshippers.

16:3 The Second Vial

The second vial is poured out upon the sea with the result that the sea becomes as blood and every living soul in the sea dies. The area of the judgment is similar to that of the second trumpet where one-third of the sea is turned to blood and one-third of the sea creatures die. Here the judgment is universal.

16:4-7 The Third Vial

The third judgment turns the water and rivers into blood. At this point John hears one described as "the angel of the waters" deliver a justification of God for this judgment. This reference further reveals the remarkable variety of ministries assigned to angels as recorded in Revelation. The angel declares that because men have shed the blood of saints and prophets, God is righteous in judging them in kind in that they are given blood to drink. Christ Himself declares it will be a time of trouble without precedent (Matt. 24:21).

The statement by the angel is confirmed by another voice out of the altar - another angel who declares that God, who is almighty, true, and righteous, manifests these attributes in His divine judgments. Combining the judgments of the second and third vials, it appears that all water is turned into blood, constituting a universal testimony to all men that God will avenge His martyred saints.

16:8-9 The Fourth Vial

In the fourth trumpet the judgment extends to the third part of the sun, moon and stars, resulting in the darkening of a third part of the day and of the night. By contrast, the fourth vial relates only to the sun and increases rather than decreases the sun's intensity with the result that men are scorched with fire. The divine judgment thus inflicted apparently upon the entire Earth, does not bring men to repentance but only increases their blasphemy, even though they recognize that the plague comes from the God whom they reject. Because the article "the" is added to men as in verses 2, 5 and 6 (the literal Greek has "the" in verse 9), this implies that saints in this period who are true believers will not suffer this plague.

16:10-11 The Fifth Vial

The fifth judgment is directed to the throne of the beast and his subjects. The result of the judgment is darkness, pain, and the accumulated effect of the preceding judgment when sores were inflicted as in the first vial. The "seat of the beast" is more accurately "the throne of the beast." This is probably the first beast of Revelation 13. The wicked in their suffering are declared to gnaw their tongues for pain, a picture of severe agony. Again, we have the sad note that they blasphemed God as the author of their judgments and did not repent of their deeds. The Scriptures clearly refute the notion that wicked men will quickly repent when faced with catastrophic warnings of judgment.

16:12-16 The Sixth Vial

The sixth vial has occasioned more comment on the part of expositors than any of the preceding vials. As the sixth vial is poured out, its particular objective is the great Euphrates River. As the result of the judgment, the water of the river is dried up and the way of the kings of the East is thereby prepared. My belief is that the great Euphrates River is actually dried up, thereby preparing for an invasion from the East (Isa. 11:15; Zech. 10:11).

The word "East" can be taken as "sunrising," referring to Oriental rulers who will descend upon the Middle East in connection with the final world conflict described a few verses later.

In verses 13-16 John has an additional vision introduced by the phrase, "I saw." In his vision he sees three unclean spirits like frogs in appearance coming out of the mouth of the dragon and out of the mouth of the beast and out of the mouth of the false prophet (12:9; 13:1-8, 11-18). These spirits are specified in verse 14 as spirits of demons (*daimonion*). These spirits are declared to work miracles (13:12-15) and are commissioned to gather the kings of the entire Earth to the battle described as "the battle of the great day of God Almighty."

The utterance of verse 15 is a direct quotation from God Himself. The expressions are used of a sudden, unexpected coming which result in judgment or loss on the part of the person overtaken (Matt. 24:43; Luke 12:39; II Pet. 3:10; I Thes. 5:2, 4). The saints will be protected from spiritual nakedness at the coming of the Lord. The saints in view here are evidently those still on Earth who have been able to escape martyrdom even though remaining true to the Lord.

The area for this great battle is called Armageddon. It relates to the "Mount of Megiddo located adjacent to the plain of Megiddo to the west and the large plain of Esdralen to the northeast."

16:17-21 The Seventh Vial

The vial of the seventh angel is declared to be poured out into the air and the resulting action is catastrophic. It is accompanied by a great voice out of the Temple in Heaven and from the throne stating in emphatic terms, "It is done." In the Greek the statement is one word in the perfect tense, indicating action accomplished.

There has been speculation as to why this vial should be poured into the air, inasmuch as Satan as the prince of the power of the air has already been cast down from Heaven. The fact that Satan has been cast out of the third Heaven does not mean that he still does not have great power in the atmospheric heavens which are here in view.

As in the case of the final seal and the seventh trumpet (8:5; 11:19) the final vial is introduced by the sound of voices, thundering, lightening, and a great earthquake. The earthquake is declared to be greater than any previous earthquake. The Earth literally convulses as the times of the Gentiles come to an end.

Verse 19 declares that "the great city" is split into "three parts" and that the other cities of the world fall. The question has been raised as to the reference to the great city, inasmuch as Babylon is specifically mentioned later in the verse. In Rev. 11:8 Jerusalem is referred to as "the great city." It is also clear that great topographical changes will take place around Jerusalem in connection with the judgments at the end of the age (Zech. 14:4). Identifying the "great city" as Jerusalem seems justified. Note that the "great city" is not completely destroyed.

Babylon, however, according to Scripture, is destined to be completely destroyed. I personally believe this Babylon is a reference to Rome. In any case, Babylon is the special object of God's divine judgment. This is the final judgment of the wicked city.

Not only does every city of the world come under terrible judgment as a result of the great earthquake, but the Scriptures also indicate great changes in the topography of the entire world. The sweeping statement is made in verse 20 that every island is affected and mountains disappear (6:14). Such a judgment undoubtedly causes great loss of life and disruption of such world organization as may have remained up to this time.

In addition to mentioning the great earthquake which is primary in divine judgments, verse 21 records a great hail with every stone weighing about a talent (100 lbs.). Try to consider the great devastation this will do to the Earth.

Although the judgment and demonstration of the power of God are great, men are still unrepentant, and verse 21 concludes with the sad statement that "men blasphemed God because of the plague of the hail, for the plague thereof was exceeding great." Chronologically the next event is that prophesied in 19:11 where Christ Himself descends from Heaven to take over His kingdom on Earth.

Revelation Chapter Seventeen

"The Destruction of Ecclesiastical Babylon"

Chapters 17 and 18 of Revelation are dedicated to the description of the final destruction of Babylon in both its ecclesiastical and political forms. It is evident from these chapters that the events described therein, especially those in chapter 17 occur at the beginning of the Great Tribulation. The revelation is given to John, however, subsequent to the revelation of the vials. It must be remembered that from John's point of view all of the events of the book of Revelation were future, and it pleased God to reveal various aspects of the future events in other than their chronological order.

Any interpretation of Revelation 17 and 18 is difficult because expositors have not agreed as to the details of their interpretation. In general, however, it is helpful to consider chapter 17 as dealing with Babylon as an ecclesiastical or spiritual entity and chapter 18 as dealing with Babylon as a political entity. It is also helpful in chapter 17 to distinguish the vision in verse 1-6 from the interpretation in verse 7-18.

17:1-2 The Invitation to View the Judgment of the Great Harlot

John is shown the vision of the destruction of Babylon, as representing false religion, by one of the seven angels which had the seven vials, and is invited to behold the judgment of a woman, the symbol of Babylon described as the great harlot. The interpretation of many waters is that these are the many nations ruled by Babylon. The woman is further described as having committed fornication. The inhabitants of the Earth are declared to have been made drunk with the wine of her fornication. The picture of the woman as utterly evil signifies spiritual adultery, portraying those who outwardly and religiously seem to be joined to the true God but who are untrue to this relationship. The symbolism of spiritual adultery is not ordinarily used of heathen nations who know not God, but always of people who outwardly carry the name of God while actually worshipping and serving other gods. The concept of spiritual adultery is frequently used in describing the apostasy of Israel (Ezek. chapters 16 and 23; all of Hosea). In the New Testament the church is viewed as a virgin destined to be joined to her husband in the future (II Cor. 11:2), but she is warned against spiritual adultery (James 4:4).

The alliance of the apostate church with the political powers of the world during this future period of time not only debauches the true spiritual character of the church and compromises her testimony in every way but has the devastating effect of inducing religious drunkenness on the part of the inhabitants of the Earth.

17:3-4 The Vision of the Woman on the Beast

Accepting the invitation of the angel, John is carried away in the spirit into a place described as the wilderness. From this vantage point John is able to see the woman previously introduced as the great harlot. She is seen seated on a scarlet-colored beast which is full of the names of blasphemy and which has seven heads and ten horns. The scarlet beast is the same as described in 13:1 where the beast is the revived Roman Empire in its character as the center of the world government of Gentile power in that day. The fact that the woman is riding the beast and is not the beast itself signifies that she represents ecclesiastical power as distinct from the beast which is the political power. Her position of riding the beast indicates that she is supported by the political power of the beast, but is in a dominant role and at least outwardly controls and directs the beast.

This situation seems to be describing the first half of the tribulation. The fact that the woman, representing the apostate church, is in such close association with the beast, which is guilty of utter blasphemy, indicates the depth to which apostasy will ultimately descend. The only form of a world church recognized in the Bible is this apostate world church destined to come into power after the true church has been raptured.

The description of the woman as arrayed in purple and scarlet and decked with gold, precious stones, and pearls is all too familiar in the trappings of ecclesiastical pomp today. Purple and scarlet, symbolically so rich in their meaning when connected with true spiritual values, are here prostituted to this false religious system and designed to glory it with religious garb in contrast to the simplicity of pious adornment (I Tim. 2:9-10). The most striking aspect of her presentation, however, is that she has a golden cup in her hand described as "full of abomination and filthiness of her fornication." The Word of God does not spare words in describing the utter filthiness of this adulterous relationship in the sight of God. Few crimes in Scripture are spoken of in more unsparing terms than the crime of spiritual adultery.

17:5 The Name of the Woman

The word "mystery" is a descriptive reference to the title, not a part of the title itself as implied by the capitalization in the Authorized Version (compare 16:19 and 18:2). "Babylon the Great" is probably not a reference to Babylon as a city or nation, but religious designation. The woman corresponds religiously to what Babylon was religiously. Many of the pagan rites of Babylon crept into the early church and were largely responsible for the corruption of the Roman church. This is made clear by the title "mother of harlots and abominations of the Earth."

17:6-7 The Woman Drunken with the Blood of Martyrs

The woman is pictured not only as the source of all evil in apostate Christendom but also as the one who is actively engaged in the persecution of true saints. Her wickedness in this regard is demonstrated by the description that she is drunken with the blood of the saints and with the blood of the martyrs of Jesus. The history of the church demonstrated that apostate Christendom is unsparing in its persecution of those who attempt to maintain a true faith in Jesus Christ. As John contemplates the woman, he records "I wonder with great admiration (literally wonder)."

The angel, perceiving that John wonders at what he sees, states that he will declare the mystery of the woman and of the beast. He does so, however, by describing the beast first in detail, then the woman and subsequent action relating to her. Few passages in Revelation have been the subject of more dispute among scholars than this passage to follow. Great care must be exercised in determining precisely the component parts of the divine revelation herein given.

17:8 The Origin of the Beast

The beast is explained chronologically as "that which was, is not, and is about to ascend from the abyss to go into perdition." The "bottomless pit" (*abyssos*) is the home of Satan and demons and indicates that the power of the political empire is satanic in its origin as is plainly seen in 13:4. The word "perdition" (*apoleia*) means "eternal domination." The overwhelming satanic power of the final political empire of the world will be most convincing to great masses of mankind.

There is confusion on the part of many between the description of Satan (9:11; 11:7; 13:3) and this beast of 17:8. The solution to this problem is that there is an identification of Satan with the future world ruler and identification of the world ruler with his world government. Each of these three entities is described as a beast. Only Satan himself comes from the Abyss, but the world power which he promotes is entirely satanic in its power and to this extent is identified with Satan. It is the beast as the world government which is revived. The man who is the world ruler, however, has power and great authority given to him by Satan.

17:9-11 The Seven Heads of the Beast

John further saw this woman sitting upon a scarlet beast full of names of blasphemy, having seven heads and ten horns. This beast is the same described in chapter 13. The Revelator describes the "seven heads" which are "seven mountains" on which the woman sits.

A mountain, or prominent elevation on the surface of the Earth, is one of the common scriptural images, or representatives of a kingdom, regal dominion, empire or established authority (Psa. 30:7; Jer. 51:25; Dan. 2:35). This is exactly the sense in which the angel uses the word here, as he himself tells us. He adds to his statement "and they are seven kings," or "personified kingdoms."

The woman is not an empire any more than the church is an empire. She rides upon empires, kings, and powers of the world, and inspires, leads and controls them; but she herself is not one of them, and is above all of them so that they count her, and are bewitched and governed by her - governed by the lure of her fornication. This woman is longer-lived than any one empire. We have seen that she bears the name of Babylon, and is not destroyed until the day of judgment. The seven imperial mountains on which she rides must therefore fill up the whole interval. Seven is itself the number of perfect fullness and completion. The reference here is to kings, to mountains of temporal dominion, to empires.

Of these seven regal mountains, John was told "the five are fallen," - passed away, their day was over; "the one is," that is, the one was standing at that moment and was in power; "the other is not yet come, and when he shall come, he must continue a little time." What regal power was at the time John wrote? Obviously it was the Roman Empire. There were five which had already run their course and passed away. They were Greece, Persia, Babylon, Assyria and Egypt. Obviously the one in power during the tribulation will be the revised Roman Empire since five have passed away and the sixth one is the Roman Empire and the seventh one had not come. Thus we are brought to the identification of these seven world powers as being the seven mountain kings which stretch from the beginning of our present world to the end of it.

Daniel makes the number less; but he started with his own time and looked only forward. Here the account looks backward as well as forward. That which is first in Daniel is third here, and that which is sixth here is fourth in Daniel. Only in the starting point is there any difference.

By these great powers then, filling up the whole interval of world's history, this great Harlot is said to be carried. It is not upon one alone, nor upon any particular number of them, but upon all of them. These seven powers support the woman as their joy and pride; and she accepts and uses them, and sways their administration and rides in glory by means of them. This is the picture explained by the angel. History shows that each of these kingdoms was a lover and supporter of organized falsehood in religion, the patrons of idolatry, the foster friends of all kinds of spiritual harlotry. It requires but a glance at history to see that spiritual harlotry has even been the particular pet and delight of the beast - powers of time.

The final form of world government that "is not yet come" and will continue only "a short time," symbolized by the eighth beast itself, is the world empire of the Great Tribulation time. The revived Roman Empire which will be in sway immediately after the rapture of the church, will move into a world empire that continues a short time and is destroyed by Jesus Christ at His coming to Earth.

17:12-14 The Ten Horns of the Beast

Further detail is given concerning the final stage of the world empire as having a nucleus of ten kings apparently joined in a confederacy represented by the ten horns. These kings are kings that rule simultaneously at the end time. This is the form the revived Roman Empire takes as it becomes a world empire. The ten horns' rule as kings are subject to that of the beast itself, and their sphere of power is brief. They are further described as making war with the Lamb, a reference to the Lord Jesus Christ, and their ultimate defeat by the Lamb.

17:15 The Explanation of the Waters

In the first verse of the chapter the harlot is seen sitting upon many waters. Here the description of the waters and their meaning are given as referring to people, multitudes, nations and tongues. The situation described here is one of great political power on the part of the beast. The meaning of the water is given here because "water" elsewhere in Revelation should generally be taken literally. Here when water is used as a symbol, the symbol is explained.

17:16-18 The Destruction of the Woman

Verse 16 reveals a most remarkable development in the vision which is also the climax and the purpose of the preceding description. Here the ten horns, seen as ten kings, destroy the woman riding the beast in a most graphic action. The original text indicates that both the ten horns and the beast combine in this effort. The most accurate translation is "the ten horns and the beast." The destruction of the harlot reduces all her pomp and gorgeous robes to naught. She is stripped of them, her flesh is eaten, and she is burned with fire.

The time of this event is approximately at the middle of the seven years tribulation. During the first half of the seven years, apostate Christendom lowers and establishes its power over all the world. During this period there is a measure of religious freedom as indicated by the fact that the Jews are allowed to worship and renew their sacrifices (Dan. 9:27). However, the triumph of the ecumenical movement is simultaneous with the final effort. All religions of the world, apart from true faith in Christ, gather in one great world church.

However, with the beginning of the second half of the week, the ruler of the revived Roman Empire, who is the political head of the world empire and is himself designated also as "the beast," is able to proclaim himself dictator of the whole world. He therefore destroys the world church and substitutes for this ecclesiastical apostasy the final form of wickedness in the area of religion, the worship of himself.

The divine judgment inflicted upon apostate Christendom follows a pattern which can be observed in other judgments upon wicked nations and ungodly rulers. Ancient Babylon was used to bring affliction upon the people of Israel, as were also Assyria and Egypt. But in due time the same nations who inflicted divine judgment were themselves the object of God's wrath. The principle involved is plainly stated in verse 17. Their action, though inspired by a blasphemous attempt to institute a world religion utterly contrary to divine revelation, nevertheless fulfills God's will that the kingdoms of this world should come under the domain of the beast in fulfillment of prophecy until the end of the age.

At the close of the chapter, the woman is again identified with the great city which reigned over the kings of the Earth, referring to the ecclesiastical power and control of the political that has its climax at the end of the age. This is obviously a reference to "Babylon" as to her nature and influence rather than the specific city itself. According to verse 5 the city is a mystery, not Babylon itself.

Revelation Chapter Eighteen

"The Fall of Babylon"

18:1-3 The Fall of Babylon Announced

The opening phrase of chapter 18 "after these things" marks a later revelation than given in chapter 17. John declares, "I saw another angel come down from Heaven." The angel in chapter 18 is different from the angel of 17:1. The term "another" makes clear that this angel is the same in kind as the angel of 17:1. The fact that the angel has great power and that the Earth is lighted with the glory of the angel lead to the conclusion that the angel is delegated to do a great work on behalf of God. The announcement declares that "Babylon the great is fallen." The verb for "is fallen" is found in the aorist tense, indicating a sudden event viewed as completed. This is constructed such to show (in relation to chapter 17) two separate parts of the fall, answering to the two aspects in which Babylon is contemplated — in chapter 17 as an ecclesiastical system — in chapter 18 as a political system.

The downfall of Babylon in 18:2 is followed by its becoming a habitation for demons, and a prison for every evil spirit and the cage for every unclean and hateful bird. This abandonment of destroyed Babylon to demons is a divine judgment stemming from the utter wickedness of the inhabitants described in verse 3. Babylon in her political character has had evil relationships with "all nations" described as "fornication." In this, they have been led by the rulers, "the kings of the Earth." The resulting evil association has made the merchants of the Earth rich. The wealth originally collected through the influence of the apostate church is taken over by the political system in the Great Tribulation which with universal political power is able to exploit to the full its accumulation of wealth.

18:4-5 A Call to Separation from Babylon

As John contemplates the announcement of the fall of Babylon, he hears another voice from Heaven addressing the people of God giving instruction to come out of Babylon (Jer. 51:45; 50:4-9; 51:6). The purpose of leaving Babylon is twofold (1) By separation from her they will not partake of her sin, (2) they will not have her plagues inflicted on them (16:17-21).

In verse 5 the sins of Babylon are declared to reach to the heavens with the result that God remembers, that is, judges her iniquities. The fact that her sins have reached (*kolco*, literally "cemented together as bricks in a building) unto Heaven is an allusion to the tower of Babel which began the wicked career of Babylon (Gen. 11:5-9).

18:6-8

In keeping with the enormity of her sin, the voice from Heaven now calls on God to reward Babylon even as she rewarded the people of God. The verb "reward" (*apodidomi*) means literally "to pay a debt" or "to give back that which is due."

The normal law of retribution, however, is here doubled in recognition of the enormity of the sin of Babylon. In keeping with this principle, the cup of iniquity which Babylon filled is now to be filled twice with the measure of her judgment. There is no mercy found in the utter apostasy found in Babylon in all her phases of operation.

The expression "lived deliciously" (*estreniasen*) means "to be wanton" or "to revel" and comes from a word meaning "hardhearted" or "strong." her willful sin against God is now to be rewarded with torment and sorrow. The torment (*basanismon*) refers to trial by torture with its resultant mental anguish and grief. The destruction from the Lord, according to verse 8, will come in one day in the form of plagues, death, mourning, and famine, resulting in her utter destruction by fire. Her vaunted strength is not compared to the power of God. The fact that her judgment comes in one day, emphasized in the Greek by being placed first in the sentence, is reminiscent of the fall of Babylon in Daniel 5, which fell in the same hour that the finger traced its condemning words upon the wall.

18:9-10 The Lament of the Kings of the Earth

The destruction of Babylon in its political and economic aspects described in the preceding verses is now the subject of a lament by the kings of the Earth. The time here is the second coming of Christ at the end of the Great Tribulation. Some believe that ancient Babylon is to be rebuilt as the capital of the world empire in the Great Tribulation period and that this chapter refers to rebuilt Ancient Babylon rather than the revised Roman Empire. I reject that theory because of statements in Isa. 13:19-22 and Jer. 51:24-26, 61-64.

The twofold lament involved in the words "bewail" and "lament" indicates to vocally lament and to beat the breast. It is reminiscent of the hopeless wailing of those who mourn the passing of loved ones.

18:11-19 The Lament of the Merchants of the Earth

The economic character of Babylon is indicated in the fact that merchants also weep and mourn for her. Their grief is occasioned by their loss of trade with her. The rich and varied character of the merchandise is itemized in verses 12 and 13, beginning with precious stones and costly metals characteristic of wealth and luxury. Next in line are the fine fabrics used in their clothing. Precious stones, versatile metals, and fine fabrics which constituted the wealth of the ancient world are here itemized as the treasure of Babylon in the hour of her destruction. The luxury of their apparel is matched by the rich furnishings in their homes including articles of thyine and other precious wood, ivory, brass, iron, and marble. Thyine was a fragrant wood corresponding to cypress and was used for furnishings in Roman times along with other precious metals.

In verse 13 expensive perfumes and spices are mentioned. The last luxury item to be listed is frankincense. All of these could be afforded only the wealthy. Next is mentioned the abundance of foods. The word "beasts" in verse 13 probably refers to cattle. The combined picture is one of complex abandonment to the wealth of this world and total disregard for God who gave it.

18:20 Rejoicing in Heaven Over the Fall of Babylon

In contrast to the grief overtaking worldly rulers and merchants by the destruction of Babylon, those in Heaven, who are mentioned later in

19:1, are called upon to rejoice at the righteous judgment of God. The address is to "the saints and the apostles and the prophets" rather than to the "holy apostles," with the article repeated each time. The expression "hath avenged" is literally "God hath judged your judgment on them," thus bringing to bear upon Babylon the righteous recompense for her martyrdom of the saints. It is another case where the righteous ultimately triumph as victory follows suffering.

18:21-24 The Utter Destruction of Babylon

John in his vision now sees a "mighty angel" throw a stone like a great millstone into the sea, portraying the violent downfall of the great city. The angel now enlarges on the cessation of activity in the great city. That which characterized its life and featured its luxurious existence, such as the voices of harpers and musicians, of pipers and trumpeters, who added to the fanfare and public display of both the religious and political Babylon, is now silent. Similarly, the fine craftsmen who produced the ultimate in luxurious goods are no longer to be found. The sound of the millstone grinding out the grain is silent. The very silence of Babylon is a testimony to God's devastating judgment.

Here too was the blood of martyred prophets and saints. Babylon is declared to be guilty of the blood of prophets and saints, reference in part to the martyrs of the Great Tribulation.

Revelation Chapter Nineteen

"The Second Coming of Christ"

19:1-3 The Alleluia of the Saints in Heaven

In response to the invitation of 18:20 John hears "a great voice of much people in Heaven." The chronological relationship of these experiences is obvious with the voice in Heaven following the destruction of Babylon in all its forms.

The reference to "much people" is to the same group as in 7:9 where a "great multitude is a translation of precisely the same Greek words. The multitude is heard saying "Alleluia." The four instances of "alleluia" in the New Testament are found in this chapter (19:1, 3, 4, 6). The saints here speak with a "loud voice." In addition to the introductory alleluia they express praise to the Lord in three great words: salvation, glory and power. The first of the three terms signified deliverance, the second God's moral glory in judgment, and the third His might displayed in the execution of the judgment upon the harlot. The article occurs before each of the words: "the salvation, and the glory, and the power of our God."

The judgments of God are declared to be true and righteous. God is praised for having judged the great harlot and having avenged the blood of His servants shed by her hand. The ascription of praise is followed by a second alleluia and the statement that the smoke of Babylon will continue to rise forever. This is a reference to the perpetual judgment of the people who engaged in her wicked deeds.

19:4 The Alleluia of the Twenty-Four Elders

The twenty-four elders first introduced in chapter 4 along with the four living creatures then fall down and add their "Amen, Alleluia." These 24 elders represent the people of God before the days of Christ and the church since the cross.

19:5-6 The Final Alleluia of the Great Multitude

Joining the praise of the tribulation saints, the twenty-four elders, and the four beasts, a voice is now heard coming out of the throne calling upon the servants of God to praise the Lord. It is probable that this is a voice of an angel rather than the voice of God or the voice of the saints. The occasion for the praise of God is His judgment against wicked men who have oppressed the people of God. The expression "his servants" does not refer to a particular group such as the tribulation saints, but rather to "all ye His servants." In other words, this is an occasion for every true servant of God to praise the Lord. The verb "PRAISE" is in the present tense and therefore a command to "keep on praising the Lord."

In antiphonal response to this call to praise, John hears the voice of the great multitude, that is, the same as in verse 1, accompanied by the majestic sound of many waters and mighty thundering, saying for the fourth time in this passage, "Alleluia: for the Lord God omnipotent reigneth."

19:7-8 The Marriage Supper of the Lamb Announced

The great multitude now announces a major feature of the Lord's reign upon Earth, namely, His marriage to His bride. As to where the marriage supper will take place, there are two schools of thought that I will present by quoting two scholars on the matter — you take your choice.

1. William R. Newell: "Where is the marriage, with its attending marriage supper, celebrated? The answer can only be - in Heaven; for the scene is wholly heavenly. No one can read verse 6 without coming to this conclusion."
2. John F. Walvoord: "If this occurs at the end of the Great Tribulation which is immediately climaxed and succeeded by the second coming of Christ, the more normal presumption would be that the supper would take place on Earth in connection with the second coming to the Earth itself."

The marriage symbolism is beautifully fulfilled in the relationship of Christ to His church. The wedding contract is consummated at the time the church is redeemed. Every true Christian is joined to Christ in a legal marriage. When Christ comes for His church at the rapture, the second phase of the wedding is fulfilled, namely, the Bridegroom goes to receive His bride. The third phase then follows, that is, the wedding feast: Here it is significant to note that the bride is already the wife of the Lamb, that is, the bridegroom has already come for His bride prior to 19:11-16. This happened at the rapture. That which is here announced is not the wedding union, but the wedding feast. The literal interpretation of verse 7 from the Greek is "for the marriage-feast of the Lamb is come."

In verse 8 a beautiful picture is drawn of the holiness and righteousness of the church in that hour, for the bride is described as arrayed in "fine linen, clean and white." We are not left to imagine what this means, for the interpretation is given: "for the fine linen is the righteousness of saints" (Eph. 5:26-27).

19:9-10 The Blessedness of Those Called to the Marriage Supper

Following the praise of the Lord and the announcement of the marriage of the Lamb by the multitude, John is now instructed to write that those who are invited to the marriage supper are truly blessed. The angel speaking the words of verse 9 is apparently the same one who on other occasions had informed John that he should write. This fourth beatitude of the book is enforced by the statement "These are the true sayings of God." So awesome is the revelation that John falls at the feet of the Angel in an attitude of worship (v. 10). Such a reaction is not appropriate for an angel, and John is rebuked with the statement that the one speaking is "thy fellow-servant, and of thy brethren that have the testimony of Jesus." The command "Worship God" means that only God should be worshipped.

The concluding phrase of verse 10 is most significant: "The testimony of Jesus is the spirit of prophecy." This means that prophecy at its very heart is designed to unfold the beauty and loveliness of our Lord and Savior Jesus Christ. In this present age; therefore, the Spirit of God is not only to glorify Christ but to show believers things to come as they relate to His person and majesty (John 16:13-15). Christ is not only the major theme of Scripture but also the central them of prophecy.

At this point in the book of Revelation the climax of the revelation is reached with the presentation of Jesus Christ as the glorified King of kings and Lord of lords. The revelation of Jesus Christ presented in the book of Revelation is in contrast to the Christ of the Gospels where He is revealed in rejection, humiliation, suffering and death. His return is to be one of triumph, glory, sovereignty, and majesty. How poverty-stricken is any Christian theology which minimizes the second coming of Christ and how limited the Christian hope which does not include the glorious climax to God's announced program of exalting His Son and putting all creation under His control.

19:11-13 The Revelation of the King of Kings

This passage contains one of the most graphic pictures of the second coming of Christ to be found anywhere in Scripture. Even a casual study should make evident the remarkable contrast between this event and the rapture of the church. At the rapture Christ meets His own in the air, and there is not evidence of immediate judgment upon the Earth. By contrast, Christ here is coming to Earth with the specific purpose of bringing divine judgment and establishing His righteous rule. Many Scriptures in both Old and New Testaments anticipate this scene (Zech. 14:3-4; Matt. 24:27-31).

As is made clear in these prophecies, the second coming of Christ will be a glorious event which all the world will behold, both believers and unbelievers. It is compared to the lightening that shines from the east to the west, in other words, illuminating the whole Heaven. The second coming will be preceded by the sun being darkened and the moon not giving her light, stars falling from Heaven, and other phenomena not only mentioned in Matt. 24 but vividly revealed in the Revelation. The climax to all these events will be the return of Christ Himself in the clouds of Heaven with power and great glory and accompanied by the saints. The final revelation of this event is found in Revelation 19.

The dramatic presentation of this awe-inspiring scene is introduced by John's statement, "I saw Heaven opened." In the vision he beholds a person who can be no other than the Lord Jesus Christ on a white horse. The opening of the heavens is dramatic in itself and to this is added the symbolism of a rider on a white horse drawn from the custom of the conquerors riding on a white horse as a sign of victory or triumph. Now the true King of kings and Lord of lords is going to triumph over those who blasphemously assumed control over the world. The titles given here to Christ are in keeping with the divine judgment which follows. He is declared to be faithful and true, and to judge and make war in righteousness.

In verse 12 His eyes are as a flame of fire, a term previously used to describe Christ in 1:14 and 2:18. This speaks of His righteous judgment upon sin. His head is crowned with many crowns, or diadems, the symbol of sovereignty. He possesses a name which no man knows, as yet unrevealed. His vesture is declared to be "dipped in blood" as if anticipating the bloodshed to come (Isa. 63:2-3; Rev. 14:20). Christ as the slain Lamb in Revelation speaks of redemption by blood; here blood represents divine judgment upon wicked men. The name given to Christ in verse 13 is "The Word of God." The Word of God, who according to John 1:1-3 is the Creator, is here also the Judge of Men.

19:14-16 The Coming of the King of Kings

Accompanying Christ at His Second Coming are those described as "the armies which were in Heaven." Some have tried to limit this "army" to the church alone. There is no reason, however, to limit this army to the church. I am convinced that this army consists of all saints plus the holy angels. The spectacle of Christ on a white horse with a vesture dipped in blood accompanied by innumerable heavenly beings clothed in fine linen is a demonstration that now at long last the filthy, blasphemous situation in Earth is going to be wiped clean with a divine judgment of tremendous character.

A further description is given of Christ, adding to the picture of divine judgment. Out of His mouth goes a sharp sword, which will be used to smite the nations and bring them under His rule. Here the word "sword" is used symbolically to represent words with which Christ will smite the nations and establish His absolute rule (Isa. 11:4).

The divine act of judgment is also described in verse 15 in the words, "he treadeth the winepress of the fierceness and wrath of Almighty God" (Isa. 63:1-6). All of these passages point to the sad conclusion that in the day of judgment it is too late for men to expect the mercy of God. The scene of awful judgment which comes from this background is in flat contradiction to the modern point of view that God is dominated entirely by His attribute of love.

The conclusion reveals that on His vesture, previously described as dipped in blood, and also on His thigh a name is written, "King of Kings, and Lord of Lords." Here at last has come One who has right to rule the Earth, One whose power and majesty will demonstrate His authority as

He brings to bear His sovereign judgment on a wicked world. God will indeed break the nations with a rod of iron and dash them in pieces and given the uttermost parts of the Earth to His Son as His rightful possessions.

19:17-19 The Battle of the Great Day of God Almighty

Following the vision of Jesus Christ and His return to Earth, the Apostle John sees an angel standing in the sun. Though some have taken this a very unusual phenomenon, the most natural explanation is that the angel is standing in the light of the sun with the angel himself shining with even greater brilliance. The message of the angel is addressed to the fowls that fly in the midst of Heaven (literally "in mid-Heaven"). The birds are invited to gather themselves to the supper of the great God. These birds are invited to eat the flesh of those killed in the battle - all the army of the beast. Every class of man with his horses is mentioned in this final judgment of world powers (Matt. 24:28).

19:20 The Doom of the Beast and the False Prophet

The consummation of the battle with victory for Christ and the armies of Heaven is described in verse 20. The beast of Revelation 13:1-10 is taken and with him the false prophet the second beast of Rev. 13:11-16. The false prophet is identified as the one who wrought miracles and deceived them that received the mark of the beast. The doom of the beast. and the false prophet culminates in their being cast alive into the lake of fire burning with brimstone.

19:21 The Doom of the Army of the Beast

In bringing to conclusion the battle of the great day of God Almighty, those that killed in the first stage of the conflict and in the capture of the beast and the false prophet are now put to death. The evidence seems to show that the entire army of the wicked are killed. This act of judgment seems to be exercised by the immediate power of Christ rather than by the armies which accompany Him. There is no evidence that the armies of the Earth prevail in any sense against the armies of Heaven, but there is total defeat of man at the height of his satanic power when brought into conflict with the omnipotence of God. The chapter concludes with a graphic note that all the fowls were filled with their flesh.

Revelation Chapter Twenty

"The Reign of Christ"

This is one of the great chapters of the Bible. It presents in summary the tremendous series of events which relate to the millennial reign of Christ on Earth. In this future period of one thousand years, many expositors believe that hundreds of Old Testament prophecies will be fulfilled, such as that of Jer. 23:5-6. The millennium is an aspect of God's theocratic program, a fulfillment of the promise given to David that his kingdom and throne would continue forever over the house of Israel. The millennium is a period in which Christ will literally reign on Earth as its supreme political leader and that the many promises of the Old Testament relating to a kingdom on Earth in which Israel will be prominent and Gentiles will be blessed will have complete and literal fulfillment.

20:1-3 The Binding of Satan

The next phase of the prophetic program is introduced by another vision of an angel. As John witnesses the scene, he observes the angel coming down from Heaven possessing the key to "the bottomless pit," that is, "the abyss" (9:1, 2, 11; Luke 8.31; Rom. 10:7). This is the home of demons and unclean spirits. The angel is also observed to have a great chain in his hands. In verse 2 the angel is seen laying hold of Satan and binding him for 1,000 years after which, in verse 3, Satan is cast into the abyss and the door is shut. A seal is placed upon Satan himself making it impossible for him to deceive the nations until a thousand years have elapsed, after which, the angel declares Satan must be loosed for a little while. Whatever the character of the chain, the obvious teaching of the passage is that the action is so designed as to render Satan inactive. In this age Satan and his demons are very active, and increasing in their activity as the time draws shorter. But, during the millennium, there will be no satanic activity.

20:4

The interpretation of most Premillenial theologians is that "they sat on them" includes Christ and all the saints related to Him including both Church and Old Testament saints (Rev. 22:5). Specific mention is made to those described as "beheaded for the witness of Jesus, and for the word of God, and which had not worshipped the beast, neither his image, neither had received his mark upon their foreheads, nor in their hands." The description fits only one class of saints, namely, the tribulation saints who in refusing to worship the beast are martyred. Here we learn that they were beheaded, first, for their positive witness for Christ and the Word of God; second, because they refuse to worship the beast and receive his mark.

These who were special objects of Satan's hatred and the beast's persecution are now exalted, rewarded and blessed. They are declared to have "lived and reigned with Christ a thousand years." The expression "they lived" implies that they are resurrected and live again (John 11:25). It is evident from this passage that others will share places of prominent rule with the church as the Body of Christ in the millennial kingdom as is also revealed in verse 6.

The most important truth introduced in verse 4 is the evident fact that a thousand years separate the resurrection of the martyred dead from the resurrection of the wicked dead.

20:5-6 The First Resurrection

In order to clarify the exact distinctions observed in this passage, John mentions now that in contrast to the martyred dead raised at this time, the rest of the dead do not live again until the thousand years are finished. The resurrection at the beginning of the millennium is therefore characterized as the "first resurrection." It doesn't mean the first one ever, but the first one in connection with the millennium. This is the resurrection of the tribulation saints that were martyred. There were other resurrections before this:

1. Jesus (I Cor. 15:20)
2. At the crucifixion (Matt. 27:52-53)
3. At the rapture (for believers) (I Thes. 4:15-17)

In describing the resurrection of the saints here, the word for resurrection (*anastasis*) is used about forty other times in the New Testament. This word is used for bodily resurrection.

A further question can be raised concerning the special mention of the martyred dead of the tribulation. In view of the fact that they are publicly humiliated and suffer as no preceding generation of saints have suffered, so God selects them for public triumph on the occasion of the establishment of His kingdom in the Earth.

The blessedness of those who take part in the first resurrection regardless of classification is summarized in verse 6 in the words "Blessed and holy is he that hath part in the first resurrection." Their estate is a happy and holy one. They are delivered from the power of the second death; and are given the privilege of reigning with Christ for the thousand years. If the church is offered the special place of being the Bride of Christ (and she is) - and reigning in this sense, then other people will also reign and enjoy privileges and rewards in a different sense.

The main burden of the passage, however, is to demonstrate beyond any question that there will be a thousand year period between the resurrection of the righteous and the wicked.

20:7-9 The Loosing of Satan and the Final Revolt

Before considering the climax of the thousand years, a brief survey of the Scripture bearing upon the millennial kingdom will serve to emphasize and justify the literal interpretation of the thousand years (Isa. 2:2-4; 11:4-9; Psa. 72). From these passages we see:

1. Jerusalem will be the capital of the millennial kingdom.
2. War will be no more.
3. The righteous reign of Christ.
4. The peace and tranquillity of His kingdom.
5. Israel will be in prominence (Ezek. 20:34-38).

John passes quickly over all these details as if it is unnecessary to repeat them and takes us directly to the conclusion of the millennial kingdom when Satan again is loosed from his prison.

On being relieved from his confinement, Satan loses no times in resuming his nefarious activities and plunges into this campaign to deceive the nations of the Earth again. Those who are tempted, I believe, are the descendants of the tribulation saints who survive the tribulation and enter into the millennium in their natural bodies. I believe that infants born during the millennium will live to its conclusion and will be required to make a choice between Satan and Christ at the end of the millennium when Satan is loosed for a little season. Undoubtedly the Earth is teeming with inhabitants at the conclusion of the thousand year reign of Christ. Outwardly they have been required to conform to the rule of the king and make a profession of obedience to Christ. In many cases, however, this was mere outward conformity without inward reality, and in their inexperience of real temptation they are easy victims of Satan's whiles.

In describing the nations, the term "Gog and Magog" is used without any explanation. I believe, as many of our scholars in Revelation, that the expression is used here much as we used to the term "Waterloo" to express a disastrous battle, but not related to the historic origin of the battle.

As the battle is joined in verse 9, the great host led by Satan and coming from all directions encompasses the camp of the saints. Apparently Christ permits the army to assemble and encircle the capital city. No sooner has the army of Satan been assembled than fire comes down from God out of Heaven, and the besiegers are destroyed, like the destruction of Sodom and Gomorrah. Thus is shattered the last vain attempt of Satan to claim a place of prominence and worship in attempting to usurp the prerogatives of God.

20:10 The Doom of Satan

Following the destruction of the armies of Satan, the devil is cast into the lake of fire. In the divine act of judgment which casts Satan into the lake of fire, he joins the beast and the false prophet who proceeded him by one thousand years. The text should be understood as teaching that both the beast and the false prophet are still in the lake of fire where Satan joins them, a thousand years after being cast into it. It is most significant that the verb "tormented" (*basanisthesontai*) is in the third person plural, indicating that the verb should be understood as having for its subjects not only Satan but also the beast and the false prophet. Thus the Word of God plainly declares that death is not annihilation and that the wicked exist forever, though in torment. The lake of fire prepared for the devil and the wicked angels is also the destiny of all who follow Satan.

20:11 The Establishment of the Great White Throne

John sees a great white throne with One sitting on it of such great majesty that Earth and Heaven flee away from before Him. Though there is no specific mention made of the person sitting on the throne, it is proper to assume that it is Christ Himself (John 5:22; II Cor. 5:10). The time is clearly at the end of the millennium in contrast to the other judgments which precede the millennium.

The most natural interpretation of the fact that Earth and Heaven flee away is that the present Earth and Heaven are destroyed and will be replaced by the new Heaven and the new Earth (Rev. 21:1; Matt. 24:35; Mark 13:31; Luke 16:17; II Pet. 3:10).

20:12-13 The Resurrection of the Wicked Dead

Before the great white throne, John sees the dead described as "small and great" standing before God awaiting their judgment. From the context it is obvious that these are the wicked dead who are not raised at the "first resurrection" (Dan. 12:2; John 5:29; Acts 24:15; Rev. 20:5). Those that appear before the throne come from all walks of life and degrees of greatness.

Their standing posture means that they are now about to be sentenced (Heb. 9:27). Their judgment is made on the basis of the books which are opened, being in two classifications. The book of life evidently refers to the roll of those who are saved and whose names were not "blotted out" of this book. The other books mentioned as plural are the divine records of their works. The dead are judged on the basis of the record and the sum of their works is not examined. Here the works are such that salvation is not the issue but rather the degree of punishment.

The absolute justice of God is revealed in the judgment of works. Even for those who have spurned the Lord Jesus Christ there is differentiation in degrees of wickedness and apparently variation in punishment. There are forty-two instances in Scripture where man is said to be judged according to his works (not for salvation but for degrees of punishment or reward). The book of life is introduced as the deciding factor as to where they will spend eternity.

In verse 13 the resurrection of the wicked dead is described, with special mention of those who are raised from the sea where they did not have normal burial. Those who died normal deaths and went to Hell are also presented at this judgment. The closing clause of verse 13 has an important Greek construction. "They" is the third person plural for the verb, but "every" is a first person singular, meaning "they were judged each man." The meaning is that while they are judged as a group, the resulting judgment, nevertheless is individual.

20:14-15 The Lake of Fire

The summary judgment is pronounced that "death and Hell were cast into the lake of fire." This is described as "the second death," which stands in antithesis to the first resurrection, or the eternal state of bliss enjoyed by the saved. The basis of the judgment is declared in verse 15 to be whether their names were found written in the book of life. The word "found" connotes the careful search of the records to be sure that no mistake has been made. Their ultimate destiny of eternal punishment is not because God wished it, but because they would not come to God for the grace which He freely offered.

Let it be clearly understood that the "lake of fire" is not for final annihilation of the wicked, but for eternal punishment (20:10). The fact of eternal punishment is not limited to Revelation, for Christ Himself speaks of the destiny of the wicked in many places (Matt. 13:42; 25:41, 46, etc.).

Revelation Chapter Twenty-One

"The New Heaven and the New Earth"

21:1 The New Heaven and the New Earth Presented

Following the judgment of the great white throne depicted in the closing verses of chapter 20 John's attention is next directed to the new Heaven and the new Earth which replace the old Heaven and the old Earth which fled away (20:11). The new Heaven and the new Earth presented here are evidently not simply the old Heaven and Earth renovated, but an act of new creation. No description is given of either the new Heaven or new Earth in verse 1 except for the statement "there was no more sea." Most of the Earth is now covered with water, but the new Earth will have no bodies of water except for the river mentioned in verse 2 of this chapter. The eternal state is clearly indicated in the absence of sea, for frequent mention of bodies of water occur in millennial passages (Psa. 72:8; Isa. 11:9; Ezek. 47:10; Zech. 9:10; 14:18).

21:2 First Vision of the New Jerusalem

Now John's attention is immediately directed to that which is central in the vision, "the holy city, new Jerusalem, coming down from God out of Heaven, prepared as a bride adorned for her husband." Most important is the fact that the city is declared to come down from God out of Heaven. In the Greek, the expression "out of Heaven" precedes the phrase "from God," just the reverse of the Authorized Version order. Nothing is said about the new Jerusalem being created at this point and the language seems to imply that it has been in existence in Heaven prior to this event (John 14:2).

I now desire to postulate an idea which is mine, but which I believe to be true concerning the "new Jerusalem." It is possible that the New Jerusalem is in existence throughout the millennial reign of Christ. It is also possible that it is a satellite city suspended over the Earth during the thousand-year reign of Christ as the dwelling place of resurrected and translated saints who also have access to the earthly scene. This explains to me the difficult problem of the dwelling place of resurrected and translated beings on Earth during a period in which men are still in their natural bodies and living ordinary lives. I feel the new Jerusalem is withdrawn from the earthly scene in connection with the destruction of the old Earth, and later comes down to the new Earth. As presented in Rev. 21 and 22, however, the new Jerusalem is not seen as it may have existed in the past, but as it will be seen in eternity future.

The only description of the new Jerusalem given in verse 2 is embodied in the phrase "prepared as a bride adorned for her husband." Some scholars say that this description of the new Jerusalem is the description of the church, and say that the new Jerusalem isn't literally a city, but represents the church. The subsequent description of the new Jerusalem in this chapter makes plain that saints of all ages are involved and that what we have here is not the church per se but a city having the freshness and beauty of a bride adorned for marriage to her husband.

21:3-4 God to Dwell with Men

John now hears a great voice from Heaven giving the spiritual significance of the scene. The fact that the voice is "a great voice," is a connotation that the subsequent revelation is important and authoritative. The voice declares that "the tabernacle of God is with men." This states that God is now present with men in the new Earth and in the new Jerusalem.

The presence of God assures an entirely new state of things for those who inhabit the new Jerusalem. In contrast to any former suffering and trials, God is now going to wipe away every fear from their eyes. Other aspects of human sorrow will also pass away; such as death, sorrow, crying, or pain. As the close of verse 4 suggests, these former things have passed away.

21:5-6 All Things Made New

And now the one sitting upon the throne speaks. An announcement is made that, "I make all things new." The word "new" (*kainos*) means to be both new in character and new in the sense of recently made. John is so astounded by the fast revelation of events that he has to be reminded to "write for these words are true and faithful." Verse 6 is a reference to the work accomplished throughout the whole drama of human history prior to the eternal state. This statement "It is done, I am Alpha and

Omega, the beginning and the end," does not mean that there are no future works of God but that a major work has been brought to completion and that the works now relating to the eternal state are beginning.

21:7-8 The Blessings of the Overcomer

Another promise now extended to the glorified saints described as overcomers ("born-again ones") (all notes on seven churches—Ch. 2 and 3) is that they shall inherit all things. Here the generous provision is made that they shall inherit "all things" rather than some particular aspect of the divine provision. Promises to overcomers are included in the messages to the seven churches and are anticipated in I Cor. 3:21-23.

In contrast to the abundant blessings on the child of God is the sad inheritance of unbelief outlines in verse 8, whose destiny is to be burned with fire and brimstone, which is the second death. While there is further mention of the fate of the unsaved later in the book of Revelation, this is the last mention of the lake of fire and of the second death specifically.

21:9-11 The New Jerusalem as the Home of the Bride

And now John is invited by one of the seven angels who had poured out the seven vials of the wrath of God to behold the bride, the Lamb's wife. Since a city is not a bride nor a wife, the truth here represents a city which is the dwelling place of the bride, and because of it being the dwelling place of the bride it is compared to a bride for beauty and is intimately related to Jesus Christ the Lamb.

Of major importance are the facts that John actually saw a city, that this city was inhabited by saints of all ages, and that God Himself was present in it. It is called "His bride" because it contains His bride, the church, and because its beauty looks as if it were a bride adorned for her husband.

Responding to the angel's invitation, John is carried away in spirit to a great and high mountain. From that standpoint of being able to see everything, John sees the holy city, the new Jerusalem descending out of Heaven. In verse 11 a general description of the new Jerusalem is given. The city is characterized as having "the glory of God."

The city is ablaze with light compared to the brightness of a precious stone such as jasper, and clear as crystal. The mention of this stone which is costly to men but used lavishly in the new Jerusalem (21:19) is designed to manifest the glory of God. Later in the passage (v. 23) the fact is revealed that the city does not originate its light or radiance, but all illumination comes from the Lamb.

21:12-14 The Wall and the Gates of the City

After giving the general appearance of the city, John now itemizes the specific details. The saints in the new Heaven and the new Earth will have as their home precisely such a city, glorious in every aspect, reaching to tremendous heights into the new Heaven, and embodying characteristics to remind them of their spiritual heritage.

Verse 12 is the wall of the city, described as "great and high." In the wall are twelve gates guarded by twelve angels and inscribed with the names of the twelve tribes of Israel. In keeping with the square shape of the city, the gates are located, three of each of the four sides as specified in verse 13. In the description of the new Jerusalem twelve is very prominent as seen in the twelve gates and twelve angels in this passage, the twelve tribes of Israel (21:12), twelve foundations (21:14), twelve apostles (21:14), twelve pearls (21:21), and twelve kinds of fruit (22:2). The naming of the gates probably correspond to Ezek. 48:31-34.

Also prominent in connection with the wall and the gates are twelve foundations inscribed with the names of the twelve apostles of the Lamb. This is to signify that the church also has a major part in God's economy in the new Jerusalem, along with all other saints and the holy angels.

21:15-17 The Dimensions of the City

And now the angel comes to measure the dimensions of the city. Using a reed, a measure of about ten feet long, the unit of measure common among the Jews, he measures the city, its gates and its walls. The angel finds that the city is square - twelve thousand furlongs. Since a furlong is 582 feet, the measured distance in the city is about 1,350 miles.

According to verse 16, the tremendous dimension of the city's length and breadth is equaled by its height which towers an equal distance into Heaven. The twelve foundations indicate that the city will be in twelve "tiers" at about 112 miles apart. These large dimensions would be proper if it is to be the residence of the saved of all ages.

In addition to the measuring the city itself, the angel measures the wall, which is 144 cubits or 216 feet high. The closing statement implies that whether man or angel measured it, the measurement would be the same.

21:18-21 The Beauty of the City

With the dimension of the city graphically given, John next describes the glory of the city. The wall is said to be of jasper in keeping with verse 11. The city as a whole is portrayed as made of pure gold like clear glass. Employing the language of semblance, John is endeavoring to give a description of a scene which in most respects transcends earthly experience. The constant mention of transparency indicates that the city is designed to transmit the glory of God in the form of light without hindrance.

Attention is next directed to the foundation of the city which is said to be garnished with all kinds of precious stones. These layers of precious stones for foundations are:

1. Jasper - clear and brilliant
2. Sapphire - blue in color, hard as diamond
3. Chalcedony - an agate stone, sky blue with stripes
4. Emerald - a bright green
5. Sordoyx - a red and white stone
6. Sardius - a reddish honey color
7. Chrysolite - a transparent golden color
8. Beryl - sea-green color
9. Topaz - yellow-green color
10. Chrysoprasus - another shade of green
11. Jacinth - violet in color
12. Amethyst - purple in color

The general picture here described by John is one of unmistakable beauty, designed to reflect the glory of God in a spectrum of brilliant color. The light of the city within shining through those various colors of the foundations and wall forms a scene of dazzling beauty in keeping with the glory of God and the beauty of His holiness.

Built in the walls are the twelve gates described as each being made of one huge pearl, leading to the streets of the city described as pure gold — transparent as glass.

21:22 The Exclusion of the Temple

John, as he searches the city, finds no temple therein. This is in sharp contrast to the Old Testament times and to the millennial situation where a temple is built for the worship of God. Here the Scripture indicates that the Lord God Himself and the Lamb are the temple of the new city. No longer is the structure necessary, for the saints are in the immediate presence of the Lord with no need for an earthly mediator.

21:23-24 The Light of the City

In contrast to the millennial Earth and all preceding history of man, the new Jerusalem does not need the light of the sun or the moon, for God Himself is the source of light in the city. The new Jerusalem is distinguished by the things that are missing - no temple - no sacrifice - no sun - no moon - no darkness - no gates shut - no abomination. That God Himself should be the light of the city is entirely in keeping with many passages in the Old Testament, and the New Testament stating that Jesus is the light (John 1:7-9; 3:19; 8:12; 12:35).

In verse 24 the nations of the saved as well as kings of the Earth are declared to walk in the light of it and bring their glory and honor into it. The meaning is not that political entities will enter into the new Jerusalem, but rather those who are saved Gentiles, Israel (or OT saints) and all others who belong to God will be in the new city.

21:25-27 Access to the City

A further word is given concerning the fact that the gates of the city are never shut, because in the city there is continuous day. The brilliant light of the city dispels any possible darkness. Believers in their glorified bodies need no rest; and their lives are full of continuous activity like the holy angels. Again in verse 26 the indication is that the glory of the nations themselves come into the city. This is another emphasis that it will be the saved Gentiles, Old Testament saints, and all who belong to God.

Verse 27 indicates plainly that nothing will ever enter the city which is in any sense evil, as only those whose names are written in the Lamb's book of life are eligible to enter. This will be a perfect environment in contrast to the centuries of human sin, and the saints will enjoy this perfect situation through eternity.

Revelation Chapter Twenty-Two

"Concluding Exhortation"

22:1 The River of the Water of Life

As a provision for the saints and in keeping with the complete holiness and purity of the heavenly city, John sees a pure river of the water of life, clear as crystal, coming out of the throne of God and of the Lamb. The river corresponds to the present believers experience of the outflow of the Spirit and eternal life. The throne is indicated as that of both God and the Lamb. This confirms that Christ is still on the throne in the eternal state, though the throne has a different character than during His rule over the Earth during the Millennium.

22:2 The Tree of Life

The visual picture presented in that the river of life flows down through the middle of the city, and the tree is large enough to span the city, so that the river is in the midst of the street and the tree is on both sides of the river. It would appear that the pure river of the water of life is not a broad body but a clear stream sufficiently narrow to allow for this arrangement.

The tree of life seems to have reference to a similar tree in the Garden of Eden (Gen. 3:22, 24). Its character is revealed as being such that if Adam and Eve had eaten of the tree of life, physical death would have been an impossibility. The tree in the new Jerusalem seems to have a similar quality. It provides leaves described as "for the healing of the nation." It also bears fruit once every month. This fruit seems to be different in kind each month for twelve months.

The word for "healing" (*therapein*) can be as easily translated "health giving." In other words, the leaves of the tree promote the enjoyment of life in the new Jerusalem, and are not for correcting ills which do not exist.

22:3 The Throne of God

To emphasize the blessedness of the new situation, verse 3 states that there is no more curse. This broad statement is justified by the fact that the throne of God and of the Lamb shall be in the new Jerusalem, and His servants will give themselves to serve Him unceasingly. What greater privilege can saints have in the eternal state than being servants of the Lord? Who would want to be perpetuated into eternal idleness and uselessness? This is a picture of blessedness in service rather than arduous toil.

22:4-5 The Blessedness of Fellowship

The blessedness of the servants' state is further declared in the fact that "they shall see His (the Lord's) face." Immediate access to the glory of God will characterize the saints of the eternal state. Further, His name is declared to be in their foreheads indicating that they belong to Him.

Once again in verse 5, John repeats the fact that there will be no night there and no need of a light, for God is the light of the city. Those who are His servants know the blessed privilege of reigning forever. Christ continue for all eternity as King of kings and Lord of lords.

22:6-7 The Certainty of the Blessed Hope

The angel goes on to remind John, in words similar to Rev. 1:1, that the God of the holy prophets has sent His angel to show His servants through the Apostle John the events which will occur. The phrase "shortly be done" literally translated is "do something quickly." The thought is that when the action comes, it will be sudden.

In verse 7 the message is that when Jesus comes, it will be "quickly." The blessing of God is especially pronounced on those who keep the sayings of the prophecies of this book. This verse contains the sixth of the seven Beatitudes found in Revelation. How ironical it is that this final book of the Bible, more neglected and misinterpreted than any other book, should carry these special notes of promised blessing to those who properly regard its promises and divine revelation.

22:8-9 John Worships Before the Angel

The tremendous impression given to John by these revelations finally overwhelm him. He falls down at the feet of the angel to worship him.

But, he is rebuked by the angel who informs him that he is John's fellow servant and should be classified with John and not worshipped. "WORSHIP GOD" (aorist imperative) - in all acts of worship - worship God only.

22:10-11 Command to Proclaim the Prophecy

John is commanded not to seal the sayings of the prophecies but rather to proclaim them. Time was at hand for them to be revealed. As the prophecy of the book of Revelation was unfolded, it was intended to be revealed, and now the proper season for this revelation was at hand.

Verse 11 is saying that if the prophecies of this book of Revelation are rejected and people remain unmoved, there is no other message that will work. If the warnings of this book aren't sufficient, there is no more that God has to say. The revelation will also cause the righteous to pursue righteousness and the holy will pursue holiness.

22:12 The Blessed Hope and Assurance of Reward

Here the "come quickly" is in the present tense connoting that when He does come, it will be quickly. This is a promise that the Lord is bring His reward when He comes. This verse has in view the judgment seat of Christ (II Cor. 5:10:11). Everyone will be rewarded (not saved) according to their works.

22:13-16 The Majesty of the Eternal Christ

It is Christ who is speaking here in these verses. Christ again repeats that He is Alpha and Omega, which is interpreted as meaning the beginning and the end, the first and the last. The three pairs of titles given in verse 13 all connote the same truth, that Christ is the beginning and source of all things as well as the goal and consummation of all things.

Verse 14 has an unfortunate translation in "they that do his commandments." The better and older manuscripts have "they that wash their robes." Since obeying His commandments is not the ground on which eternal life is bestowed (John 5:24). I also agree with the translation "they that wash their robes." These believers have the right to enter through gates of the city and have access to the tree of life.

By contrast, unbelievers are characterized as being excluded and are described as "dogs, and sorcerers, and prostitutes, and murderers, and idolaters, and whosoever maketh a life." The reference to dogs refers not to the animal but to men of low character (Phil. 3:2). The issue is not that they have at some time committed sins of this character, but rather that these are settled characteristics of their lives from which they were not delivered although the grace of God made possible their deliverance.

In verse 16, the term "I Jesus" is used to indicate that the Lord Jesus Christ has sent His angel to testify the truth of this book to John and to deliver the book to the churches.

Additional titles ascribed to Christ are "the root and offspring of David (Isa. 11:1) and "the bright and morning star" (Num. 24:17, Rev. 2:28). The reference to the churches is also significant. This is the first time the word "Church" has occurred since the letters to the seven churches in Rev. 2 and 3.

22:17 The Invitation of the Spirit and the Bride

As the book of Revelation comes toward its close, a special invitation is given by the Spirit and the bride. This refers to the Holy Spirit and the Church. In light of the prophetic word, the invitation to all is given - "come." The invitation to come is an urgent command, for the day will arrive when it is too late. Now is the day of grace.

22:18-20 The Final Testimony of Christ

The urgency of the final command is supported by the solemn testimony of Christ Himself in verse 18 concerning the sacred character of the prophecy which has been given. Warning is extended that if any man add to these things, God will inflict upon him the plague written in the book, and if any man take away from the prophecy of the book, God will take away his part out of the book of life and from the things written in the book including the holy city. No one can dare add to the Word of God except in blatant unbelief and denial that the word is indeed God's own message to man. The point of these two verses is that a child of God who loves Him will recognize and believe the word of God. Anyone who would dare "add to" or "subtract from" this prophecy would only be someone who did not know God personally. Although there are numerous interpretations to this Revelation, I have never seen a believer who desired to "add to" or "take from" this Revelation. This passage assumes that a child of God would never tamper with God's word.

The final testimony of the book is yet another repetition of the promise of Christ's return in a quick way - "Surely I come quickly." The word "surely" is used to clench the certainty of His coming. John begins his own prayer response by the announcement: "Even so, come Lord Jesus."

22:21 Benediction

As John closes this remarkable book of which he is the human writer, he uses the phrase so familiar in Paul's epistles, a benediction that the grace of the Lord will be upon His readers. This final book of the Scriptures which began with the revelation of Jesus Christ ends with a prayer that His grace might be with those who have witnessed these scenes through John's pen. With John I say, "Even so, come, Lord Jesus."

The author may be contacted as follows:

Dr. William "Bill" Oakley
P.O. Box 1633
Dyersburg, TN 38025
Phone: (901) 285-7710
E-Mail: w.p.oakley@worldnet.att.net